Tales of
Fort Thomas

Tales of Fort Thomas

A.J. Bass

To Ben:

Thank you for making me slow down.

A Note from the Author

When I began writing The Fort Thomas Series, the story I ended up with (or will end up with once the remaining books of the series are out) was bigger and more complex than I had initially imagined. Because of this, a lot of the little, personal stories I had in my head were pushed out of the picture; there was just no way to fit it all in without the story becoming a busy mess.

Tales of Fort Thomas is my way of including some of the little stories I had to cut. As a collection of stories, I'm able to give each one the attention it deserves, as opposed to just a glancing mention. If you've followed me on social media, you may recognize some of these stories, only now they're all spit-shined and gussied up for their official debut.

Not all the stories take place after *Paige's Story* ends. "Funeral for a Fish," the first story in this collection, takes place right in the middle of the story. "Ghosts of Christmas Past" recounts events that happened long before *Paige's Story* even begins. Consider *Tales of Fort Thomas* a companion to *Paige's Story*.

That said, if you're thinking about buying this book and haven't read *Paige's Story*, you may want to put this back and grab it first... or grab both. Or don't, and just read whatever your little heart desires. I'm not your supervisor. But if I were, I'd tell you to save this one for later, not because you won't enjoy it, but because you'll appreciate it more that way. Think of it as literary pudding. And we all know what Pink Floyd says about having your pudding first.

Funeral for a Fish

The apartment door slid shut behind Jake much faster and much louder than he was prepared for. With a guilty cringe he called, "Sorry," across the apartment but got no response. He turned back to the door and glared at it. He had hoped that after three weeks the thing would work its kinks out, but so far, no such luck. He'd just have to call maintenance and have them look at it. Maybe they could switch it out for an old-fashioned knob and hinges door like they used to have. Sighing, he put his briefcase on the kitchen bar, crossed the living room, and started down the hall. He stopped to glare at the off-color patch on the wall where workers had repaired it a few weeks back. They had run out of the exact shade of off-white and went with 'close enough'. Close enough. Close enough to stand out like a clown at a funeral. He thought about what that patch job was covering and shook his head.

"Broken doors and bullet holes," he said to himself. "Sounds like a country song."

As he passed Paige's room, he heard the unmistakable sound of video games coming from inside and that was reassurance enough things were fine. He went into the bathroom and downed what some might consider an excessive amount of ibuprofen before going into his and Anita's room. Once inside, he took off his shoes and threw himself onto the bed. The pillows were cold and felt great against his aching head which, at the moment, felt like a family of bad-tempered wasps had taken up residence inside it.

Ever since Alpha put him and Anita on their current top-secret project, the days seemed to all blend together into one caffeine-addled, stress-laden, hellscape. It was like finals week back in college right down to the Chinese take-out food at all hours, except this time there was much more riding on his efforts than a test score.

Sleep tugged at him, and he threw himself at it— the softness of the mattress, the gentle breeze from the overhead fan, the sudden vibrating under his butt.

Jake's eyes shot open, and he shifted so he could reach his back pocket.

"It hasn't even been half an hour, 'Nita. I just laid down," he groaned, not bothering to look at the ID before he answered his cell.

"Oh, my apologies Dr. Bryan, I was unaware—"

Jake shot up at the sound of Alpha's voice. "I'm sorry, Alpha. I thought you were Anita."

There was a pause followed by an uncertain, "Would you like me to be?"

Jake gave a tired chuckle, "No, I definitely would not."

Alpha gave a chuckle of his own, "That's good. I don't think I'd be able to manage her level of colorful language."

Jake nodded and moved to the side of the bed. "Few can." He slipped his shoes back on and stood up, assuming more work was on the way. "Now, what can I do for you?"

There was another pause, then Alpha replied, "A civilian call was routed here from the Rutherford County courthouse in Murfreesboro Tennessee. It got bounced through almost every department here until it somehow got to me."

Jake stroked his beard, his exhaustion giving way to curiosity. "What's it regarding?"

"A civilian family with a pair of synthetics had one wake up recently."

"And they want to sell the Jane to Section? That's the acquisitions de—"

"No, no," Alpha interrupted, "They don't want to sell him; that's just it. They have questions about integration."

"Integration?"

"Yes, they want to integrate him into the family unit. I figured if anyone knew about living with us Janes on that level it would be your family. Could you spare some time to answer a few questions?"

Jake smiled and glanced into the hall toward Paige's room. Alpha certainly hit the nail on the head with that one. "Of course I can. Let me transfer you to the living room and get a video conference on the big screen."

One minute later Jake was seated on the sofa looking at a man about his age on the TV monitor. He was blonde, with rough looking skin that was used to being exposed to the elements. His work shirt—Jake assumed it was a work shirt—was a well-worn, flannel, button-down shirt that was dotted with flecks of...grass? Hay? Was it too early in the year for hay? He didn't know.

"Dr. Bryan?" the man on the screen asked in a heavy drawl. "I really appreciate you talkin' to me. I was about to give up if I got transferred again."

"It's no trouble. Director Alpha—" Behind him, the apartment door slammed shut then reopened and slammed again twice more in rapid succession.

Jake glanced over his shoulder and saw Paige just arriving home from school. "Jesus Christ! Can we please get this door fixed before it crushes someone?"

"Paige?" He turned back to the screen, "Sorry. It's my daughter." The man gave an understanding nod and Jake turned back toward the kitchen where Paige was rooting through the refrigerator. "Hey, kiddo, I'm on a conference call here. Can you maybe keep it down and ix-nay on the anguage-lay?"

"What the hell's an anguage-lay?" she asked as she crossed the room, can of Coke in hand. Before Jake could reply, she vanished down the hall into her room.

"Sorry about that," Jake said, returning his attention to the screen. "Now, Mr.—" An ear-splitting shriek tore down the hall and through the apartment from Paige's room. Jake jumped in his seat and so did the man on the other end of the monitor.

"Ever'thing okay?" the man asked.

"I—" Jake tried to answer but was cut off again.

"You murdered Gobo!" Paige's voice roared, followed by an equally angry, though younger-sounding, reply.

"I did not!"

"Did too!"

"Did not!"

Jake felt every ounce of blood rush to his face as the accusations and subsequent denials bounced back and forth like the world's angriest game of Pong. Jake put his hand to his forehead and pinched the bridge of his nose, hoping the ibuprofen would kick in soon. "I am so—"

"It's fine, Dr. Bryan, I got a kid of my own 'bout her age. It's always somethin'. Go on'n sort it. I'll wait."

"I won't be a moment," Jake promised and dashed down the hall. As he got closer to Paige's room the argument grew more heated. This must have been what it was like when his father had to work from home when he was a boy, he thought then corrected himself. No, he was never as rowdy as Paige. This must have been what it was like for Freya and Joseph when Anita was a kid. Sometimes he wished Paige had inherited more than just his nose and hair. "What is going on here?" he asked, as he pushed the bedroom door open.

He saw Paige standing beside her bookshelf, livid. "Um, hello? Have you not heard? Anji is guilty of first-degree fishslaughter!" She turned toward the bowl on the nearby bookshelf and tapped on the glass where Gobo floated, belly up, on the surface; his long red fins dangled limply below him. "Don't worry buddy, I'll avenge you," she whispered to the dead fish.

"Anji?" Jake looked down at the little red-haired Jane seated on a beanbag chair. "Did you... You know?" He made a stabbing motion with his hand.

"No, Uncle Jake, I swear. I've been playing video games all day—"

"Neglecting him!" Paige interrupted. "It's negligent pescacide!"

"Neglect? What's to neglect? He was fine this morning just lazing at the bottom of his bowl like he's been for the last week."

"Wait," Jake interrupted, "Just lazing at the bottom of his bowl!"

Paige shrugged, somewhat calmer now, "Well, yeah. He's been kind of lazy lately, but he'd always come up to eat."

"He didn't this morning," Anji mentioned.

"Paige, just how old is Gobo, again?" Jake asked his daughter while he, likewise, tried to dig back in his memory for the information.

"I got Gobo four years ago from Grandpa Bryan as a condolence gift after Charles died." Paige crossed her arms and looked even grumpier. "Stupid window. Stupid sidewalk," she muttered.

"Please," Jake pleaded. "I have an important call to take, we are not bringing up Charles right now."

"Who's Charles?" Anji asked, curious.

Jake raised his hands to stop her when he saw Paige about to launch into a rage filled telling of the death of her robotic smart pet. "Charles is another topic for another time," he explained to Anji. Man, where was Anita when he needed her? She'd have this whole situation wrapped up before it even started. A forceful swear here, a physical threat there, and bingo-bango, crisis averted. "Paige, the average lifespan of a fish like Gobo is about 5 years, tops. If he was lethargic and not eating, I'm guessing he just died of old age. When I'm off this call we'll flush him, and that will be that."

Paige's eyes flared and Jake knew he'd stepped on a landmine. "Flush him?! Flush him?! How dare you even suggest such a thing!" she fumed. "No. Gobo was a good fish. He deserves better. I'm going to get a hold of Alpha and arrange an honor guard. It's the least I can do."

Jake sighed and gave up. "Fine. Do what you have to do. But please let me get to this call." He shut the door and left Paige to her funeral planning.

"Get yer kids all sorted?" the blonde-haired man asked pleasantly over the monitor.

"For the most part," Jake replied. "My niece is staying with us for a bit." He used the cover story they had come up with just after Anji's arrival. "And well, sometimes they get at each other's throats."

"I see. Well, give 'em my condolences for the goldfish."

"Betta. Gobo was a betta fish."

"Oh, I see. Well, all the same."

"Much appreciated. Now," Jake said, straightening up. "How can I be of service to you today, Mr. Caldwell?"

"Well," Jake watched him shift in his seat and furrow his brow. "I'm not sure how to put this in a way that won't sound ridiculous."

"Mr. Caldwell—"

"Derrick is fine."

"Derrick, my daughter is planning a funeral for a betta fish that includes full military honors. Whatever it is that's on your mind, I think I can take it."

"Alright, alright, that's fair," Derrick conceded. "It's about one of my farm hands, ya see."

"Yes, Alpha informed me Jane recently awakened one of your synthetics, and you're wanting to integrate him into the family, correct?"

"When ya say it like that it sounds so clinical," Derrick replied. "But yeah, we're awful fond of him and want to make him part of the family— his sister, too if the same ever happens to her." He paused again to collect his thoughts. "What I wanna know is, is it possible?"

"I'm sorry, I don't think I follow."

"Is it possible? Y'know, to be a normal family when one of the members… isn't? It's just we're in a small town, and we've got the only two synthetics in, shoot, I dunno a fifty-mile radius at least, let alone the town itself."

"You're worried about backlash against your family?"

Derrick shook his head. "No. I mean, I'm sure there'll be talk, but that ain't my concern. My concern is whether or not he'll be happy. Like I said, he's the only one of his kind 'round here. That's gotta be isolatin' and lonely."

"Has he been behaving strangely since waking up?"

Derrick considered the question. "He's quieter now. Before he… well, he was always real talkative. Always smilin'—"

"If I may interject; before, he was following a program. Most synthetics are designed to be talkative and happy. He's not following the program anymore. He's going to experience and react to things like a human would, and right now, everything is new and intense. He'll need time to adjust.

"I suppose that makes sense," Derrick sighed. "I'm just concerned. He seems lost in his own head most of the time. I can't imagine what he's thinkin', and when I ask, he makes up some answer that I know is bullshit— pardon my language." He shook his head and rubbed the back of his neck. He seemed stressed, and Jake didn't blame him. "I mean, he's a good kid— can I call him that? A kid? I mean, he's full grown… Jesus, I don't even know the words I'm s'posed to use."

Jake smiled. He sympathized with the situation, and had he not made synthetics his career he wouldn't know all the correct verbiage and protocol either. What he found heartening was Derrick's desire and willingness to learn. If he was willing to call all over hell and back on this Jane's behalf, he was certain he'd be mastering social protocol in no time.

He was about to reply when Paige crossed the living room. "Hey, do we have any black fabric? We need mourning bands." She opened a cabinet in the kitchen and grabbed a bag of potato chips.

"Not to my knowledge, kiddo," Jake called over his shoulder then turned back to Derrick. "I understand your concern, I really do. And I wish I could tell you it's going to be easy for him and for your family." He thought about the fights Paige got into at school with other kids and about the protesters who used to picket outside the gates. "I know you say you're not worried, but you have to be prepared for pushback from your community. And he's got to be prepared for it too. On top of that, you must be prepared for the possibility that he won't want to stay with you. Granted, you can make him stay— legally; he is still your property."

"Nah," Derrick disagreed, "He stopped bein' property as soon as he woke up. We won't hold him prisoner if he don't wanna stay."

Another argument erupted from the bedroom. "Hey, gimme the laptop back!" Anji exclaimed.

"No! I need it!" Paige snapped. "Use yours!"

"That is mine! What do you need it for— tiny coffins? Are you serious?"

"Look at my face, Anji, I'm super fucking serious."

"Language!" Jake shouted down the hall and went back to the call, "She gets it from her mother."

"They always do," Derrick agreed. "My boy's just as bad sometimes."

"Hey, Alpha," Paige crossed the living room again, this time on her cell phone. "I don't know if you've heard but there's been a tragic death in the family."

"Oh my god! It's just a fish! Get over it!" Anji called from the bedroom.

"You get over it!" Paige hollered back as she returned the chips to the cupboard.

"I am over it!"

"Yeah, no, sorry Alpha. Gobo died, and I need an honor guard, Taps, and probably like a 21-gun send off. You think Fer would do that? He likes shooting guns..." And, once again, she vanished into her room.

Jake shook his head and went back to the matter at hand. "My point is—"

"I'm sorry, I don't wanna be nosy," Derrick interrupted, "but did your daughter just ask Alpha—*the* Alpha—to give a funeral for a fish?"

Jake felt a laugh rise up his throat, "Yeah, I guess she just did. And, you know, he'll probably do it too."

"Are you serious?"

"Oh yeah, Alpha's fond of her that way." Jake thought for a moment. "Actually, you could say they're practically family; all of us. And I'll be honest with you Derrick, it's the best damn thing that's ever happened to us. It's not always easy, and there are people who don't understand. But, at the end of the day, we're happy, and if I may be so bold as to speak for him, I'd say Alpha's pretty happy having us in his life, too."

Derrick gave a slow nod. "Thank you, Dr. Bryan. That's very reassurin'."

"I'm happy to help. When we're done here, I'll sent you some links that should also help out with your situation." Jake said. "But right now, if it's not too much trouble, may I speak with him?"

"Of course. But why?"

"Well, I'd be remiss if I didn't meet the person you're going to such great lengths for. Is it okay?"

"Well, sure. Gimme a minute." He looked down at a small hockey puck looking device on the desk, "Hey Dot, find Bourbon n' tell him to come to the office."

The hockey puck lit up bright green and a digital female voice replied, "Message sent."

A moment later, a figure appeared in the doorway just out of Jake's view. "Dot said ya wanted to see me?"

Derrick got up and moved off screen, "I do. C'mon in, son, have a seat. I got someone who wants to meet you." He pulled a desk chair over then seemed to reconsider the choice and grabbed a heavy, wooden chair.

Bourbon took a seat and looked at Jake and then to Derrick. "That him?" he asked, his voice carrying the same melodic drawl.

Derrick nodded and crouched into view, "Bourbon, I want ya to meet Dr. Bryan. He works for Section at Fort Thomas." Then he turned back to the monitor, "Thanks again, Dr. Bryan. I appreciate your time and insight."

Bourbon watched Derrick leave and close the door behind him. For a long moment Jake watched as his gaze lingered on the door. It was as though he was waiting for him to return. He seemed confused, and, if Jake didn't know better, nervous.

"Bourbon?" Jake broke the silence. "My name's Jake Bryan. It's a pleasure to meet you."

Bourbon shifted in his seat, and Jake watched the warm copper light in his eyes fade and refocus as he turned his attention to the monitor. "Howdy, Sir." He gave a hesitant smile. "Pleasure to meet ya."

For a moment Jake didn't speak, he just examined the Jane on the screen. He was broad, and solid, clearly built for hard work. He, like Derrick, was dressed in a flannel work shirt and worn blue jeans. "Is there somethin' I can help you with, Sir?" Bourbon asked, letting what little smile he wore, falter. "I ain't in trouble, am I?"

"What? No, of course you're not," Jake replied, realizing just how this conversation must seem to him. "I was just speaking with Derrick and wanted to meet you. I understand you recently experienced sudden, onset sentience as a result of the Jane virus, correct?"

"Yessir."

"Well, welcome to life in technicolor," he replied, and made sure to sound as unthreatening and upbeat as possible. "How are you adjusting?"

Bourbon's head bobbed side to side; his shaggy, blonde curls dusting his shoulders as he considered the question. "It's… loud."

"Loud?"

"Yeah, like ever'thing's comin' at me all at once. Colors are brighter, music's louder, and I notice stuff now, like the way the grass smells in the mornin' or how hot the sun is durin' the day. It's nice but sometimes too much, y'know." He paused as if to gather his next thoughts. "Sometimes, I feel real good n'excited, n' the next minute I'm worried I'm gonna get scrapped b'cause I know that I'm not like ever'body else," he said and looked down at something on the floor near him and reached for it. It took a moment for Jake to realize he was petting a fat calico cat that was rubbing against his leg.

"I assure you; no one has any intention of scrapping you."

"I know," Bourbon replied and shooed the cat toward the door. "But still, I mighta just woke up last week, but believe you me, that's plenty of time to get up to speed."

"It's an easy task when you have the internet in your head," Jake noted.

Bourbon frowned, and in a low, thoughtful voice, continued, "I know how the world sees me, and it scares me. And I know how they see me," he gestured toward the door behind him. "And that scares me, too."

Jake smiled hoping he could send some comfort through the monitor. "Why does that scare you? The Caldwells, I mean. I can understand the internet bit— it's humanity's greatest resource and a god-awful nightmare at the same time. But, as I understand it, the Caldwells would like you to join their family. I can't see what's so scary about that."

Bourbon pressed his lips together and a look of frustration and anxiety settled on his face. Having a teenage daughter, Jake was familiar with that particular cocktail of emotions. Right now, he knew Bourbon was trying to put those feelings, that were so clear on his face, into words.

"It's scary," he began, "because I barely know how to be me let alone how to be in a family. What if I screw it up? What if—"

There was the sound of footsteps rushing down the hall. "I'm going outside!" Paige declared, bolting through the living room.

Jake gave Bourbon a 'one minute' finger. "May I ask why?"

"To wait for the delivery drone. It'll be here in 20." She pressed the door control and it opened halfway then slammed shut. "Goddamned door!" She pressed the button again and it opened. "Be right back."

"Delivery drone?" Jake asked the now empty doorway.

"She used your credit card and bought a tiny coffin, Uncle Jake," Anji tattled from the hall.

"How did she—"

"She memorized the numbers," Anji answered his question before he could finish.

He sighed, time to get a new card... again. "But she has her own bank account. Why... never mind," Jake muttered to no one and turned back to Bourbon, resigned to the situation. "Young man, no one knows how to be a family. A family just is. I mean, look at this," he gestured behind him. "I have my displaced niece sharing a room with my teenage daughter who, as you may have noticed, is planning a funeral for her dead pet fish— for whom she has apparently purchased a tiny coffin. Our apartment door is a potential death trap, and my wife has been working for almost 18 hours straight. It's chaos. Every day. Not a damn one of us knows what we're doing. And yeah, sometimes we screw up. It happens. But we're happier screwing up together because whatever the problem is, we can tackle it together and overcome it together." He smiled at the screen. "So, it's okay if you're still learning. We all are. If I may paraphrase Ray Bradbury, sometimes you just have to jump off the cliff and learn how to build your wings on the way down."

"That sounds hard," Bourbon replied.

"Oh, it is. But I'll tell you, it's much easier when you're surrounded by people who care about you, and I think it's safe to say the Caldwells care a great deal about you." He leaned forward on the edge of the sofa. "I'd hug you if you were here, but you're not, so how about..." He raised his hand up to the monitor, "Internet fiver."

"You're a dork, Uncle Jake!" Anji called from the bedroom.

"Ignore her," Jake said, still offering the high five. "C'mon, don't leave me hanging. I was the coolest guy in my high school D&D group."

Bourbon raised his hand and mimicked a high five on his monitor, then put his hand down and burst into a smile a mile wide. "Coolest guy in D&D, huh?" he chuckled.

"Well, second coolest. Natalie 'Nat 20' Anderson was coolest," Jake admitted. "But it made you laugh."

"Fair 'nuff," Bourbon replied.

"I hope I've given you something to think about as you're figuring out just who and where you want to be," Jake said, happy to see his initial nervousness melt away.

Bourbon nodded, and his smile softened. He seemed thoughtful, like he was focusing on a plan as opposed to staring, confused into a mess. "Ya did. Thanks," he replied. "I'm glad I got to talk to ya, Doc."

"Same here. I'll let you get back to your day. But before we go, I just want you to know that you're going to be fine, and I'd be overjoyed to have you in my family." He watched Bourbon don another ear-to-ear grin. "Now, if you'll excuse me, I have a funeral to plan."

Girls' Night Out Part 1

The Interrogation

"ARE YOU SURE you can handle this?" Ino asked as she and Anjiko stood outside the interrogation room in the subbasement of Fort Thomas' Central Ops building.

Anjiko stole a glance at the illuminated windowpane on the wall where their suspect, a skinny human male, waited on the other side. As he waited, he alternated his gaze between the mirror on his side of the glass and the door. "Oh yeah, I got this. Easy-peasy," she said and turned toward the door. She hadn't so much as taken a step when Ino grabbed her arm.

"Are you sure?" she asked again. "Because I can go."

She could go. But, moreover, she wanted to go. The guy on the other side of that door had information she wanted— needed— and she knew she could get it much faster than her pink-haired counterpart. For, as competent as she was, Anjiko was not intimidating. Sure, she was big, bigger than her anyway, and she was strong, but sometimes the part of her that used to be Anji would come out. When that happened, it was hard to take her seriously. Ino, however, had no such problems. She could lead an interrogation and get what she needed in no time at all. Half the time, she didn't even have to Read the suspect. Just knowing she could get what she wanted at any time was usually enough to get someone to talk of their own accord.

"No, you need to stay here," Anjiko replied. "You are way too close to this. I don't want your personal involvement to cloud your judgement."

"But—"

"Don't worry. I'll get him to talk. Then we'll find whoever did this to you and take them down." She put a reassuring hand on Ino's shoulder, and the interrogation room door slid open. She stepped inside and waited until the door was closed behind her before she sat down.

The room was empty inside save for a single lightbulb hanging from a cord in the center of the room and a screen-top table with two chairs directly below the light. Seated on the chair on the far side of the table was one of the humans from the Central Ops support staff. He was dressed in the usual office casual get-up the civilian dress code mandated; his chosen brand of fashion consisting of a dark green polo shirt with his Fort Thomas digital ID badge pinned to his right breast and khaki pants.

"Levi Drywater," Anjiko began, propping her elbows up on the table and tenting her fingers. "How's it going?"

The question bounced across the table with all the grace of a fish that had just flopped out of its bowl. Her casual tone did not match her aggressive posture and devious expression.

"I- I'm sorry, Sergeant, I don't think I understand. Why am I here?" Levi asked.

Anjiko rested her chin on her fingertips. "You look nervous, Mr. Drywater. Are you nervous?"

The dispatcher, who couldn't have been more than twenty-six, shrugged as if he wanted to say, "Well, duh." but instead opted for, "The Omegas usually interrogate criminals. You guys are... well, I'm not a criminal. I'm not even a jaywalker. I—I even pay for all my own TV streaming accounts."

Anjiko flinched at the admission and momentarily lost her focus. "Wow. You do? God, that's gotta cost, like, a ton. Do you even pay extra for the ad-free versions? I mean—" she cut herself short when she realized she was rambling. *"Pull it together. Ino's counting on you. Now's not the time to be friends,"* she reminded the little girl inside her head then cleared her throat and got back on track. "You may not be a criminal, but you know one."

"I what?"

"You were at the scene of the crime, and I know you saw who did it."

The dispatcher across the table pushed his chair back and spread his arms wide, in a grand gesture of ignorance. "Did what? I have no idea what you're talking about!"

Anjiko could see the frustration on his face; he was really sticking to his guns. That was okay, so was she.

"Two days ago, at 14:00, you and one of your coworkers were in the break area, just outside our briefing room, where you saw the crime take place," she said. "I just need a name. That's all. Tell me who you were with and then you can go back to work."

"I would if I had any idea what you're talking about!"

Anjiko's fist came down hard on the table causing the lights on its interactive surface to flicker. "Quit lying!"

"I'm not!"

The chair shot out across the room as Anjiko rocketed to her feet. She leaned over the table, eyes blazing, like she was about to tackle the terrified young man. "Do you want me to go outside and get my colleague? Do you?" she asked. "Have you ever met her?" She saw Levi shake his head. Anjiko's eyes lit up at the response, and she looked alarmed. "You haven't?" Her voice was hushed now, as though she were relaying secret, lifesaving information. "Well, let me tell you something; she is creepy! When she looks at you, her optics light up and you can feel her digging around inside you. *Feel* it. And when she's done, she knows everything from the lies you're covering up to the athlete's foot you're treating."

"Th-that's not true," Levi stammered. He'd heard the stories surrounding the mysterious Omega Reader. He swallowed hard. "They're just rumors, right? I mean, I know she can do some crazy stuff, but she can't know everything."

"You sure about that?"

He was not. "I— I don't know. I just don't understand why—"

Anjiko turned around and waved at the mirror. "Hey Ino! Why don't you—"

"Okay! Okay! Yes, you're right! I was there!" Levi admitted and sank into his chair. "I was there, and I'm sorry! Just keep her away from me!"

Anjiko smiled and motioned for Ino to hold off. "Smart move. The last person she read, wound up getting divorced two weeks later. Dunno what she found," she grinned, "but it must've been juicy." She pulled her chair back over and sat down again. "Now, spill it."

"Fine. Yes, I was in the Omega's break room Wednesday with my coworker. We were looking for new headset batteries, and we figured you guys get all the good stuff, so you must have some batteries, right?"

"And who was this coworker? Give me a name."

Levi tapped the tabletop and a digital keyboard lit up on the surface. He tapped out a name and sent it to Anjiko's HUD. She read the name and nodded.

"Where can I find him?"

The dispatcher's fingers moved across the tabletop again and more info appeared in her HUD.

"There; that's his address."

Anjiko reviewed the information and, after a few long, agonizing seconds, seemed satisfied. "Thank you, Mr. Drywater. You're free to go."

Anjiko exited the room and saw Ino waiting for her.

"So? Did you get it?" she asked.

Anjiko beamed with accomplishment. "Yep. And I got an address too."

"Shall we pay him a visit?"

Anjiko shrugged, "Well, you have been saying that we're long overdue for a girls' night out."

Ino's pale face lit up. "Perfect. We'll take this monster down and—"

"And then get margaritas!"

AFTERMATH

THE FAINT YET ever-present smell of old sweat filled Paige's nose as she stood on the padded mats in the middle of the Taekwondo studio. To her left stood Kristen and Jim, the class's two senior students. To her right, a pair of brown belts. The remaining students, ranging in rank from white to blue belt, all stood in neat lines of five behind her. At the front of the room, Master Park called everyone to attention and began class.

It had been almost six months since Paige had been in class. Four long, horrible months of court hearings and being treated like a prisoner by her foster family followed by a couple more months getting settled into Alpha's house— her house now, too she supposed. Yep, the nightmare was over. She was with Alpha now, and she was fine.

She was fine.

Paige said those three words, or some variation of them, every day. Sometimes, she trumpeted them like a battle cry. Other times, she whispered them like a prayer. *"I am fine. My parents are gone, but I am fine. Things are better. The hardest part is over."*

She was well aware her use of the phrase Hardest Part indicated the existence of a less terrible but still unpleasant Harder Part, which was followed, presumably, by a final Hard Part to be dealt with before she officially hit Smooth Sailing, but she didn't like to think about that. In fact, she'd become rather adept at ignoring it altogether, opting instead to skip ahead to Smooth Sailing the same way she skipped grades back at her old school in Chicago.

She breathed in the old studio funk again, gave an affirmative nod, and reminded herself, one last time, that she was fine. Class began and Paige found it was just like riding a bike, right up until she was asked to review her newest forms— the ones she had been learning just before she was taken away by Child Protective Services. Sure, it had been a minute since she'd practiced them, but how hard could they be to remember? She was Paige Bryan; her mind was like a library, with everything carefully filed away in her cabinets and ready for her whenever she needed it. Well, at least, that's how it usually was. Now a days, though, it was more like the Thunderdome. Information went in, but it didn't often come out, and when it did, it was kind of mangled and wrong. Regardless, she stood in front of Master Park, opened her cabinets, and began her form.

The moves came without hesitation as Paige kicked and blocked with practiced precision. But, halfway through, instead of a single knife hand block, her cabinets skipped forward about three moves and told her to do a side kick instead. In an instant, Paige knew it felt wrong and she stopped. Why, of all times, did her brain have to glitch out now? Paige felt her ears go red with embarrassment. She blinked and gave her head a shake like she was trying to knock everything back into place, but it didn't work.

"Go back to your knife hand," Master Park coached. "Remember what that block turns into; a target."

"Right. Yes Ma'am," Paige said and turned her palm sideways to prepare for the punch that followed. She punched then turned to repeat the move in the opposite direction. She stopped again. That wasn't right. She stood motionless in her back-stance shuffling through her files.

They were out of order—all of them. It was like someone had come in and just scattered them all over her brain. She felt tension grip her shoulders and neck, and her heart rate accelerated. "I'm sorry. I think I'm confused. May I start over, Ma'am?"

Master Park nodded and Paige began the form again with similar results.

"Jim, Kristen, why don't you both come up and do the form with Paige. One on each side so she can have a constant reference." Jim and Kristen both got to their feet and took a place on either side of her. "On my count, begin." The three of them moved to Master Park's steady counting and this time Paige made it through the entire form without issue. The three of them were about to take their spots along the edge of the mats and let the next in line practice when Master Park called them back. "You know," she said in that patient way she had whenever she saw one of her students struggling, "a little review never hurt anyone, whether we've been away for a bit or in class every week. Why don't you all stay and do your old forms with the lower belts?"

"Yes, Ma'am," the three replied in unison and retook their spots on the floor.

Paige's insides went sour knowing she was the reason for the review. She didn't need the extra help; couldn't Master Park see that? She was just off to a rocky start. It happens. No big deal. She would have been fine if her files hadn't gotten jumbled. That was more disconcerting to her than anything. She had forgotten something. That never happened; at least not where martial arts were concerned. Yet, there she was, doing old forms, and sneaking glances at the brown belts to make sure she was on track.

The remainder of the class was filled with forms all the way back down to the white belt forms. Thankfully, those were seared into her muscle memory so deep the only way for her to forget them was to have her brain surgically removed from her skull. After forms, they all bowed and ended class. Twenty minutes later, after everyone, save for Paige and Master Park, had gone home, the front door opened and in walked Fer.

It was the first time Paige had seen him since her parents' funeral, and it took every bit of her restraint to not bolt across the floor and hug him; Fer was never much for mushy stuff like that anyway, at least not from her. Instead, she opted for some good old fashioned trash talk. "Hey, Captain Grumpy Pants, you ready to get your ass kicked?"

Fer crossed the floor to Master Park, kissed her, and sat down on a nearby chair to take off his boots. So much for not liking the mushy stuff, Paige thought, feeling more than a little grossed out at the sight; not that she wasn't happy for them. Fer and Master Park always had this weird will-they-won't-they thing going on, and she was happy they finally progressed beyond it. It was just… Fer. Yuck.

"You know," Fer said as he tugged at the laces of his boots, "I think it's just adorable that you still think you can kick my ass." He approached Paige and gave her a stiff pat on the back. "It's good to see you, Monkey. It's been real boring around here with you gone."

Paige raised an eyebrow and smirked, her frustration from earlier having all but vanished upon Fer's arrival. "Couldn't have been that boring." She nodded to each of them. "Looks like I'll have to start calling you Captain Kissy Pants now." She saw Master Park bite back a laugh and look a little red in the face. "Seriously, when did that happen?"

"About two weeks after none of your business," Fer replied, though not in an unfriendly way. "Now, come on, get ready. We've got a lot of lost time to make up for." He disappeared into the locker room to change. Paige, likewise, took off her belt and heavy uniform top, preferring to dress down to her lighter, cooler tank top.

"You ready for this, Monkey?" Fer asked when he emerged from the locker room, dressed in his usual gym shorts and t-shirt.

"You have no idea," Paige beamed, and it was true, she had been look- ing forward to this all day.

"Alright, then. Let the ass whooping be—" Fer stopped dead, as though his thought had been shot point blank. His mouth hung open mid-word and the warm, amber glow in his eyes brightened, reflecting the shock on his face.

Paige looked down at the raw, pink patches of skin peppering her arms. She was so excited to spar with him she'd forgotten about them and taken off her long sleeves, putting them on display for everyone to see. Paige watched Fer's gaze jump from scar to scar, all the way up until he reached her shoulder and saw the big one, where he stopped and just stared, wordless.

Paige felt the muscles in her shoulders tighten again, and she instinc- tively crossed her arms trying to cover herself. Everyone always stared, especially at the big one— the Big Mama Scar, she called it— the one left from the giant chunk of glass that skewered her when the Jane who killed her parents chucked her through the store window. It was the one that took well over two dozen stitches to close and still hurt when she hit it just right and itched something fierce.

Fer moved his mouth to speak, but nothing came out. Paige was famil- iar with the reaction. It was the same one Alpha had when she came trotting downstairs her first week at his house in a spaghetti-strap pajama top. She'd also experienced it from her classmates when she changed for gym class; except they didn't just stare, they whispered and commented, and that was worse. She shouldn't have expected anything different from Fer, but when she met his gaze, she didn't see pity, or disgust. There was sympathy there on that scruffy face of his; an expression which said, "Jesus, kid, I'm so sorry. Those gotta fucking hurt."

"Aaw, someone looks jealous of my badass battle damage," Paige said, forcing everyone to loosen up and smile, herself included.

Fer took the hint and, for her sake, went along with the new, lighter tone. "Badass is right," he agreed, "Those things put my little scrapes to shame." He arched his scarred eyebrow and motioned for her to follow him onto the mats, where they bowed and raised their fists. Once they were in position, Master Park put her whistle to her lips and blew, but the sound that came out wasn't the trilling, *fweet*, Paige had heard a million times before. The sound that hit Paige's ears was a scream; shrill and frightened. She blinked and for a minute, the studio was gone, and she was back at the mall. Her stomach twisted into a knot as the singular scream of the whistle became two, then four, then ten. Soon it was an entire chorus of angry shouting, cries of fear, and calls for help. The sound was so clear and horrible, Paige knew if she didn't do something it would swallow her whole, and she'd be lost forever in the noise.

Then, she blinked again, and it was gone. The noise was gone, the mall was gone, and barely a second had passed. She looked at Fer as he bobbed from side to side, waiting for her to make the first move. Paige studied his stance, found her opening, and advanced with a front kick meant for his leading knee.

"Jake! Jake! Get up!"

Paige's kick faltered as the voice of her mother rang in her ears so clear she could have been standing right behind her. Paige corrected herself and turned her failed kick into a spinning back fist to Fer's jaw.

"Somebody, help me! Please! Help me move him!" The desperate fear in her mother's voice was a punch to the gut. Paige blinked and found herself back at the crowded mall, trying to reach her mom who was on the ground hunched over her dad's limp, bloodied body like a scared animal.

Fer caught her arm with laughable ease and the next thing she knew, she was lying on the mat with him leaning over her. "Now, about that ass kicking you promised me?" he grinned and offered his hand.

The fall shocked Paige out of her… what was that exactly? A hallucination? She wasn't sure. Either way it was over, and she took Fer's hand allowing him to help her back to her feet.

"Quiet, you," she said. "I'm just knocking the rust off."

Master Park's whistle trilled once more, and Paige winced at the sound. Her pulse was racing and every fiber of her being was yelling at her to run away. She set her jaw and tried to focus. She was fine. The riot was over, and she was safe. *"The hardest part is done. I'm fine."*

This time, Fer took the lead. He thrust his fist forward and everything froze. The studio was gone again, and Paige was face to face with the Jane from the mall. She remembered the sharp, piercing pain of her wrist as it broke against his frame and the throbbing pressure that followed as it swelled. Her shoulder, where the glass cut it, felt like it was on fire. The voice of her mother filled her head; crying out as she watched her daughter fight the lethal machine in front of her.

"Paige, stop! Please, get out of here!"

Paige wasn't angry this time, though. She wasn't determined to save her parents. She knew she couldn't do it. She knew she had already failed and would fail again, and again, and again. The reality echoed through to her core until there was no courage left in her, only fear; fear of the inevitable pain her failure would always result in. The hardest part wasn't over. It was back, replaying in all its misery.

The attack was coming. She had to do something. Paige watched Fer's fist move toward her as though time had slowed. She felt dizzy and did the first thing that came to her; she raised her arms to shield her face and turned away, cowering against the blow. "No! No! Don't hit me!" She cried while in her head she heard her mother calling her name and pleading, *"Don't hurt my daughter!"*

Paige knew what would happen next. That beast would set his sights on her mom and then she, like her father, would be gone.

At the sound of Paige's cries, Fer tried to stop, but he was too close and moving too fast. The best he could do was redirect himself and hope he didn't hit her too hard. What the hell happened? She had never choked like that, not even on her first day fighting him. What's more was she knew better. She knew taking a hit from him was the last option in a long line of last options. There was no way he could stop in time. She was way too close, and he was… *"Oh, shit I'm gonna brain her."*

In a last second effort to avoid complete disaster, Fer shifted his weight and pulled his fist to the side. He didn't hit her in the head like he feared, that was a relief, but he did hit the big angry looking scar on her shoulder. Paige's agonized scream hit his ears and every ounce of his being ached with remorse.

Paige fell hard on the mat holding her shoulder, her body convulsing in great, heaving sobs. Over the sound of blood rushing in her ears, she heard Fer's voice, frantic as he dropped to his knees beside her. "Oh shit! Oh shit! Are you okay? Oh shit... Melissa!" he called. "Melissa, I need some help here!"

"What happened?" Paige felt Master Park's footsteps vibrate through the mats as she rushed toward them. "Did you hit her?"

"I don't know. I mean— yeah, I did; I didn't mean to. I went to punch and she... I'm sorry. I didn't mean to hit her, I tried to stop," Fer apologized, then leaned in closer. Paige wasn't shaking as much now, but she was still curled up in a tight ball on the mat, holding her shoulder. "Paige, are you okay?" He asked. He wanted to reach out and help her sit up, and he almost did, but thought better of it. Paige didn't respond, she just lay there on the mat, breathing in fast shallow gasps. Fer leaned in closer and saw her eyes were unfocused and distant; a million miles away seeing who knows what. "Paige," he said, exchanging a worried glance with Master Park. "I need you to talk to me or else I'm going to call an ambulance." He got nothing but a whimper in response. Whatever the hell she was seeing, it wasn't any good. "Paige, come on, please say something."

Somewhere amid the screams in her head and the pain in her shoulder Fer's voice managed to gain purchase and Paige realized she was lying on the floor, though she wasn't sure where. She blinked and with each repetition the cacophony in her head quieted. After a moment, she picked herself up off the mat into a sitting position. Her arm, all the way down to her fingertips, felt like she had been stabbed with a thousand hot needles, all radiating from the shoulder where Fer's punch landed.

"Oh, thank God," Master Park said. Her cell phone was in her hand, ready to dial 911. "Are you okay?"

Paige blinked some more, and the hard floor of the mall turned back into the Taekwondo studio. "I don't—" she said, her voice shaking. Fer and Master Park looked like they had just defused a bomb. "I don't know what happened. I heard Mom screaming, and Dad... I saw him...s-saw him all... I wanted to fight back, but I was so scared. Then, I saw the guy who— and all I could think of was how much it hurt when I… and my parents and— and the screaming…" She took a breath and tried to calm herself. "I heard my mom crying for help… she was— she was so scared. And all I could think about was how she died screaming and scared… And even though I knew it wasn't real anymore… I froze." She pulled her knees into her chest and gave into her tears again.

Fer turned to Master Park hoping he didn't look as helpless as he felt. He knew when he saw Paige again, she wouldn't be the same person as before. Just like he wasn't the same person he was back before he lost Rho. He knew. He knew how much she blamed herself, and how much she hurt inside, just like he had.

"It's okay," he said, shifting himself so he was seated on the floor beside her. "It's okay. We don't need to jump back into sparring yet. I'm not going anywhere." He didn't reach out to hug her or give her any kind of comforting touch. He felt he'd probably touched her enough at this point with his rogue punch and didn't want to push his luck. Instead, he just sat beside her and let her emotions run their course. "Melissa, can you get her some tissues?" he requested when it looked like she was calming down.

Paige wiped her tears, blew her nose, and took a few long, slow breaths. "I'm sorry," she said.

"No. No apologies needed. At least not on your end," Fer said. "I'm sorry I hit you."

Paige shook her head. "It's not your fault. You tried to stop. I'm not mad at you." She rotated her shoulder a few times to show it wasn't injured in any real way, and that seemed to satisfy him.

"Think you can get up?" He asked.

Paige nodded, and they got to their feet.

"I think you two should call it a night," Master Park suggested as they stepped off the classroom floor.

"I agree," Fer said. "C'mon Monkey, get your stuff. I'll drive you home."

About half an hour later they were back at Fort Thomas. It had been a long ride spent in silence. Every so often, Fer would glance over to check on Paige only to find her staring out the window into the dark countryside, looking like she was a million miles away again. The glossiness in her eyes told him she wasn't quite finished crying and, though it made him uncomfortable, he understood. Out of habit, Fer almost made the mistake of taking Paige to her old apartment building. Luckily, he corrected himself before she noticed. Paige did not need that kind of salt in the wound right now.

Fer pulled into the long concrete driveway in front of Alpha's house— Paige's house now too, he corrected— and saw she was still looking out the passenger window, puffy-eyed and tired. He put the Jeep into park and turned toward her. Further up the walk, the ornate front porch lamp switched on, covering the lawn in a mix of warm, yellow light and contrasting shadows.

"Hey," Fer began just as Paige's hand landed on the door handle. She turned and faced him, looking like she had been told to climb a mountain after having just run a marathon. "I want you to know what happened tonight is okay, and it's normal."

"Whatever. It's fine, Fer. I'm fine," she shrugged and went for the door again.

"No, you're not. You know how I know you're not fine?" Paige raised an eyebrow, and he continued, "I know because I wasn't fine when I lost Rho. I thought I was, and I told myself I was, but I wasn't. I was angry and confused, and I know you are too." He paused and waited for her to respond, but she just tightened her lips and gave a quick, curt nod. He sighed. He expected his words to fall on deaf ears, but it still stung. "All I'm saying is if you ever need help navigating the waters—"

"I know how to find you," Paige finished, the exhaustion in her voice was enough to make Fer tired, himself.

"I'm serious," he said. "Look, you may be an obnoxious little monkey, but you're my obnoxious little monkey, and I…" He faltered a moment when the image of her lying on the floor popped back into his head, "I just want to help. One friend to another."

Paige forced her lips into something that resembled a smile in only the vaguest sense. "Thanks, I appreciate it."

"Paige, I'm serious."

"I know you are," she said, it was like fishing line was tugging up each end of her mouth. "I'm sorry I freaked out tonight, but I'm fine now." She opened the door and got out. "Thanks for the ride."

There was motion on the porch and Fer saw Alpha in the doorway— probably investigating what the hell was holding up his daughter. He waved and Alpha returned the gesture. "Right, any time," Fer sighed and watched her make her way to the porch where Alpha ushered her into the house.

*

There were six sparrows, a male and female cardinal, and one dark-eyed junco in the tree outside Paige's history classroom. She knew this because she had been more focused on the comings and goings of the budding maple tree than her teacher's lecture on the pandemic of 2029. As she watched the birds flit from branch to branch, she replayed her conversation with Fer. Well, it was more him talking *to* her than them conversing. She wondered if he really did get what was going on in her head. Not that it mattered because she was fine. It had been almost a week since she had seen him. After their failed sparring match, he stopped showing up to class. He probably thought he was being a friend by giving her some space, but really, it just upset her. What she wanted to do was to fight and get back to the way things were. The way things were was comforting and stable. The way things were didn't hurt like this new normal did.

Outside, a second male cardinal showed up and they started fussing over the female.

"Can anyone give me three reasons why the 2029 pandemic hit the former US so hard?" Mr. Larson asked. About 10 hands shot up, but his focus landed on Paige and her birdwatching. "Miss Bryan. Why don't you give it a try?"

Paige cringed and dragged her attention back to the classroom, kicking and screaming. She gave a heavy sigh. "People were stupid, people were stupid, and people were stupid," she said, deadpan. Beside her, Nikki kicked her in the ankle and gave her one of her patented, 'girl, watch your ass' glares.

"Okay," Mr. Larson replied, keeping his general good humor about him. "Can you elaborate on the stupidity? Because there was a lot of it."

Paige shook her head and glanced back outside to see the junco had left the tree. She frowned. She liked that little bird— It was so round and squat, with its little yellow beak and beady eyes. Annoyed, she turned back to her teacher. "I don't want to elaborate on it. We hear the stories every flu season. We know what happened. The former United States took all the lessons they should have learned from the 2020 plague or, hell, even the 1918 plague and chucked them out the window in favor of being morons, and millions died as a result. Boom. The 2029 plague in a nutshell."

"Paige, I don't appreciate you taking such a flippant approach to something so tragic."

"And I don't appreciate *you* calling on *me* when my hand wasn't raised," she snapped. "But you did, so I gave you an answer. People were stupid, that's what happened! I'm not going to gussy it up for you just to make it more interesting. It was a fucking shit show. Everyone knows that."

There was a sound of rushing air as the entire class gasped. Paige rolled her eyes and felt Nikki give her another kick to the ankle and caught her, also patented, 'you done fucked up' glare. She looked back to the front of the classroom and saw Mr. Larson was also giving her a similar glare. Around her, some of the students managed to overcome their stupor and were whispering among themselves about how Paige 'just totally lost her shit.' and was 'sooo screwed.'

"I suggest you check your attitude, Miss Bryan, before you get yourself into more trouble than you're already in. I understand you've been through a lot—"

"You don't understand a damn thing. This is dumb. All of this is fucking pointless," she snapped, obliterating any further goodwill her teacher may have had.

"Alright then," Mr. Larson replied, in a tone reserved only for the most difficult of students, "If my lessons are so pointless, how about you spend the rest of the class in Principal Sagester's office."

"Already on my way," Paige mumbled, her backpack already shouldered and laptop in hand.

Outside, the birds had all flown away.

*

Alpha had seen enough TV shows and movies to know when a parent got called into the principal's office, it was never for anything good. He'd found himself in General Coffey's office on plenty of occasions, answering for his own mistakes or the mistakes of his scrappers and assumed it would be like that: a thorough recounting of the offending incident and instruction on how to rectify it. It was never fun, but it was tolerable.

He was checked in at the school by the security officer and then led through the administration office toward the principal's office where he saw Paige sitting on a chair just outside the door, pouting in that stubborn way teenagers did.

"Hey, kiddo, is everything okay?" he asked and crouched down beside the chair.

Paige didn't reply. Instead, a secretary put a hand on his shoulder and said, "Principal Sagester will see you now, Sir." Alpha got up, gave Paige one more concerned glance, then stepped into the office.

"Director Alpha," a tall man with graying hair and a sizable bald spot greeted. "I'm so sorry to pull you from your work, I'm sure you're very busy."

"No, it's fine," Alpha replied, and extended his hand. "I have assistants for a reason."

Principal Sagester smiled one of those well practiced, professional educator smiles and, after shaking his hand, invited Alpha to take a seat on the stiff office chair nearby.

"First off, my staff and I would all like to offer our sincerest condolences on the passing of Paige's parents," Sagester began, taking a seat behind his desk. "It shocked all of us and we are truly sorry for your loss." Alpha nodded his thanks and he continued, "We'd also like to congratulate you on winning your custody battle. We here at The Academy are all very much pro-synthetic rights, and we were all thrilled to hear you'd be her new guardian. She's been with you for what? A month or so now?"

Alpha nodded again, confirming his estimate, but raised a hand to stave off any further small talk. "While I appreciate the sentiments, if we could get down to brass tacks; exactly why have I been called here?"

Over the course of the next twenty minutes, Alpha was not only told the story of Paige's outburst in history class but was also informed she was missing over half of her homework assignments, her grades had taken a sudden, massive fall, and her over all attitude toward her classmates and the staff often bounced between apathy and blatant hostility depending on the day.

Alpha felt himself sinking into the chair. Each item the principal discussed felt like a weight being placed on his shoulders, and by the time the list was exhausted, he wasn't sure if he had the strength to stand.

"We understand she's been through a lot, and we're willing to work with her, but she doesn't seem to want our help, or any help for that matter."

Alpha shook his head, and he tried to formulate a reply. What could he possibly say? His mouth moved in vague motions of "How" and "Why?" but no words came. He had no idea any of this was happening. He knew she was having bad dreams, and yes, she was much more reserved, but hostile? The weight on his shoulders doubled. Not even two months in and he was already screwing it up. "Principal Sagester, I am so sorry. I was unaware of any of this. Thank you for telling me. I'll take her home and we'll sort it all out."

"I'm sure you will," he smiled, "but— and please take this as just one parent to another— humans, just like every other animal, have a biological parental instinct. It comes from our basic need to propagate our species, you know."

Alpha couldn't tell if the principal was stating a fact or trying to be funny in one of those wink-wink, nod-nod, kind of ways—propagate the species, if you know what I mean.

"Yes, I am well aware," Alpha replied.

Principal Sagester nodded and continued. "Synthetics well…" he stopped and back pedaled, "I'm not saying parental instincts aren't there, but perhaps they just take time to develop. After all, none of your kind have ever been in a position like this. We all know you weren't designed with raising children in mind, and that's not your fault. Successful parenting takes a certain level of emotional maturity and life experience. If you'd like, I can recommend some parenting classes and family counselors."

Alpha straightened up in his seat. There it was. He wasn't just a new parent. He was a defective parent because he, as far as he could tell, didn't have a need to propagate the species, thus no ingrained knowledge or desire to care for a child. He cocked his head to one side and hoped he looked as offended as he felt. Judging from Principal Sagester's reaction, he did.

"I see," he said. "While I appreciate the offer, I'll pass."

"Director Alpha, I'm sorry. I didn't mean to imply you're not fit. Like I said, we were all thrilled with the news. It's just—"

"It's just I'm not a human," he interrupted. "I'm not a human or any other type of animal for that matter. I'm a machine. As such, I've never been a child or had a parent. I am also unable to reproduce and have no innate desire to do so. So how could I possibly know, even after all my decades of life, what it's like to have common decency and concern for the well-being of someone beyond myself? Or is it just that empathy is something beyond my capability because I was built instead of born? Is that what you're saying?"

Principal Sagester didn't reply; he just sat behind his desk scrambling for ways to somehow pry his foot from his mouth, and when he found he was unable, resigned to his blunder.

Alpha stood up. "If there's nothing more you need to tell me, I'll be taking Paige home now."

*

"So, when did you plan on telling me that you're failing just about every one of your classes?" Alpha asked as the shiny black sedan drove them both back to Fort Thomas.

Paige shrugged, "I don't know; when report cards came out, I guess."

"And what's all this about you being hostile to the other students and the staff?"

"Well, as far as students go, it's really just Gwen, and she's always been the queen of West Bitchington, so I don't know why they think that's suddenly news."

"Paige." Alpha gave her a warning glare.

Paige rolled her eyes. "What? Remember when I got suspended last semester? That was her. As for the rest? Well, they keep trying to get into my business when I don't want them there." She crammed her hands into her jacket pockets and shifted beneath her seatbelt. "They keep treating me like I'm broken and that a hug and a pep talk will fix me. Point one, I'm not broken. And two, nothing is going to fix what happened. So, sorry, not sorry for telling them to take their pep talks and stick them up their asses."

"Okay, that's fair. I can understand not wanting the help of people who are, for the most part, strangers," he conceded. "But I can't allow you to keep neglecting your homework and disrespecting your teachers. If you get back on the ball now, like today, you can still salvage your grades and maybe make out with C's or low B's."

"Why?" Paige asked, turning her attention back out the window. "I doubt the ability to quote Shakespeare or identify a frog's internal organs is going to be of much use in the real world. I mean, who seriously cares?"

"I seriously care!" Alpha snapped. Paige jumped; her face was a pale moon of shock. Alpha had never raised his voice to her before. "I care," he said again, this time reining in his frustration. "Your grades in high school are what will help you get into a good college, so you should care too."

Paige gave another apathetic shrug. "Well, I don't."

Alpha bit his lips together and gave a frustrated sigh. "You don't?"

She shook her head. "What? It's not like I need good grades to join Section anyway."

Alpha's eyes went wide, and he almost choked on a laugh, "Oh, so you're joining Section, are you?"

"Yep. Last I checked, I'm still really good at repairing synthetics and kicking people's asses." She paused and rethought that last bit, recalling how she freaked out during her sparring match with Fer. Regardless, she was still a whiz at the SRC and would probably be back to giving Fer the business in no time.

"You are not joining Section," Alpha said in a nip this in the bud kind of tone.

"The hell I'm not. Someone's got to keep shit like Black Friday from happening again."

"And we will."

"Are you sure about that? Because, if I'm not mistaken, without me or my parents, you'd all still be chasing your tails wondering who the hell Joshua was and why Mirth went crazy and tried to kill me, Anjiko, and Nikki. So, forgive me if my trust in the establishment is a bit shaken." She knew she was in dangerous territory as she watched the anger on Alpha's face grow more and more pronounced, but she kept talking. "I connected the dots, and Mom and Dad found the bugs! You don't get to tell me you're handling it!"

"Hell shit it all, Paige! That is not fair!" Alpha snapped, allowing his frustration to win the moment as the car pulled into the driveway. Paige stared back at him, stunned. The raw anger in his voice was like a swift smack in the mouth that not even his clumsy swearing could soften. Alpha, likewise, saw the alarm on Paige's face and realized, while she had stepped out of line, he was the adult in the room... or in this case, the car... and forced himself to calm down. "That's not fair," he said again, calmer, but still displeased with her accusation. "Your mom and dad weren't just employees to me. They were my friends, and I miss them too. Every day I think about how I could have done something— anything— differently and saved them." The car stopped and Paige pushed the door open and got out, wanting to be as far away from Alpha as possible, as soon as possible.

"We can get through this together," he said to her as she exited the vehicle, "but only if we try. Right now, I'm doing the best I can. I just need to know you'll do the same."

Paige stood in the driveway, backpack slung over one shoulder, looking at him. He wasn't angry anymore. She was expecting him to still be angry, like her mom would have been— giving her all flavors of hell— but he wasn't. He was sad, and if she didn't know better, scared. And she was expecting to, likewise, be angry herself. She wanted to be angry. Angry at someone, anyone, just to give her emotions a target, someone else all the guilt and rage could chew on for a while. Instead, she felt the same sadness and worry she saw in Alpha. She knew he didn't deserve the horrible things she had just said to him, and part of her knew she should apologize, but she was just so tired.

"Go back to work," she said at last, her voice was calm and even. "I'll be here. If I start now, I can still turn in most of my missing work for partial credit. I can get my shit together and still pass this semester." She shut the car door and went inside.

Paige got to her room, tossed her backpack on her desk chair, and lay down on her bed with her legs still hanging over the edge. She looked up at the ceiling of her new room and watched the fan make its slow, steady rotations above her. She replayed her argument with Alpha in her head and cringed. God, she was a brat. After all, this wasn't easy for him either, but unlike her, at least Alpha was trying to make things better.

From the moment he'd taken her in, Alpha had done everything possible to make sure she was comfortable. He hired designers to come in and turn his unused guest room into an actual living space. It was cozy and full of color, with high-end decor and designer everything. It was like something from one of those home makeover shows that were always on TV. Hell, knowing Alpha, he probably hired the same people. And though it seemed completely alien, Paige had to admit, it was the coolest looking room she'd ever had.

It wasn't just her room, though. Alpha even cooked for her at least a couple nights a week when she was home, anything she wanted, from macn-cheese to pho tai. She stretched and laughed a little to herself. The pho was just supposed to be a joke; Paige's way of testing the waters. She had never had the stuff in her life but saw it on a cooking show one morning and requested it for dinner just for shits and grins, to see if he'd actually do it, and he did. He downloaded a recipe, ordered all the ingredients, and went full on Master Chef. It was so odd for her to see Alpha, the Director of Section, the most famous synthetic on the continent and probably the planet, chopping vegetables and poring over a giant stock pot, that she made a point to file the image away in her cabinets so she could keep it forever.

"I'm such an asshole," she mumbled, then grabbed Kevin and held him in front of her

face. "Why am I such an asshole, Kev?" The stuffed cat, of course, didn't reply.

After a few seconds of fruitless waiting, she put Kevin down, got up, took her laptop from her backpack, and set to work on catching herself up on her homework. It was time to get back on track.

It had been dark outside for a long time when Paige noticed the front yard lights activate and saw Alpha pull into the driveway. She looked at the time on her screen and saw it was half past midnight. *"Shit, have I been working that long?"* she asked herself and realized, no, she hadn't been working that long. She'd been spacing out and watching internet celebrities play video games that long, but not working.

As he approached the front door, a generic feminine voice spoke from the small sphere on her desk. "Alpha is home. I'm unlocking the door."

"That's fine, Kiku," Paige replied to the sphere. "Tell him I'm still in here." She heard the front door open, then close, followed by Kiku's voice downstairs relaying the message.

There was a knock, then Paige's door opened a crack. "Feeling better?" Alpha asked, waiting a moment before opening the door the rest of the way.

Paige spun around in her chair and shook her head. "I didn't get anything done," she confessed. "I tried, but it's like my brain just wants to shut down and go someplace comfortable." She nodded toward her screen where a young man was playing a horror game, declaring to his viewers that he was a 'brave boy' as he ventured down a dim hall, likely to certain doom.

"Derelict houses and killer... what is that? Fungus?"

"Mold."

"Ah. Well, if that's not the definition of comfort, I don't know what is." He smiled and Paige was relieved to see he wasn't angry. "It's okay. You've got the whole weekend ahead of you to catch up."

"But I have shifts at the SRC this weekend," Paige said.

Alpha sat down on the giant furry bean bag chair beside her desk. His eyes were bright in the dim light of the room. "Are you sure that's a good idea?" he asked, correcting his posture as he sank backward into the chair. "I'm sure Monarch will understand and make an exception to your schedule given your current situation."

"But I don't want her to make an exception for me. I want to go to work and be normal."

"I know you do, kiddo," Alpha said. "But normal isn't going to happen if you're made to redo your sophomore year." He reached out and shut the laptop. "School first. I'll contact Monarch and let her know you won't be in tomorrow."

"No. I'll do it. I'm not so pathetic as to need you to call in sick to work for me."

"I never assumed you were pathetic," Alpha said in his usual patient tone. "I was thinking more along the lines that I'm your boss's boss, and she won't give me any pushback."

Paige felt a tiny grin creep onto her face, "That's fair. But I can handle it myself. I *want* to handle it myself."

Alpha nodded and stood up, with some difficulty, from the beanbag chair. "Okay, I'll leave it to you. I'm afraid I'll be working all weekend. Unfortunately, the Omegas and the Sigmas have some very dirty work to do in The Republic of Texas."

Paige's eyes narrowed with confusion. "Why aren't the scrappers at Fort Isaac handling it? Is it that bad?"

Alpha frowned and nodded in a way that said it was, in fact, that bad.

"Wow, they need the Omegas and *all* the Sigmas?" she continued her questioning.

"Just first and second platoon."

"Still," Paige marveled, trying to deduce what could be so serious that the Texans had to call them for help. The Sigmas were engineers and tacticians, known for both their brains and brawn. They were highly respected, and most scrappers aspired to be among their ranks. The Omegas… well, they were known for kicking in doors and laying waste to anyone or anything they were up against; they were called The Game Enders for a reason, after all. Then, after a few more seconds of consideration, Paige's stomach went cold. "It's not Joshua or anything like that, is it? He's not—"

"No, no, nothing like that at all." Alpha must have noticed the apprehension on her face and reassured her, "My brother is buried under a hundred feet of rock and soil in a million pieces, according to the after-action report from the Omegas. No, the mission in Texas is altogether different."

"Still," Paige said, feeling better but still concerned as to what could require that kind of force. "Can you tell me what they're doing?"

Alpha shook his head. "Just know, if all goes well, we're going to have a lot of refugee Janes to process and place over the next few weeks."

"And if all doesn't go well?"

"Fer's in charge of the operation. It'll go fine. Now, get some sleep."

Paige nodded and Alpha closed the door behind him. Sleep? No. Not a chance. Sleeping meant nightmares and stress dreams, and she intended to put that off as long as possible. Instead, Paige grabbed her cell phone and opened a group text for Fer, Anjiko, and Ino.

"Good luck tomorrow and be safe. Kick some ass," she typed.

A few seconds later Fer replied with, *"We'll be fine, Monkey. Besides, you still owe me that ass-kicking from last week."*

A few seconds later, *"Grazie cara,"* popped up in the replies from Ino, followed immediately by a string of grinning emojis and bombs from Anjiko.

Satisfied with her replies, she opened her laptop and started her video again.

*

The next morning, Paige awakened in the same manner she always had lately, with a sudden jolt into consciousness followed by about fifteen seconds of not knowing where she was or how she got there. She blinked, trying to chase off the remainders of her most recent bad dream in which she was back at her foster family's house, locked in her room which was also part of the mall somehow. "It's fine. You're fine," she said to herself. "You're in your room at Alpha's house." She paused and corrected herself. "Home. You're in your room at home."

It felt so strange to say. This place didn't feel like home. Not like her house back in Chicago or even her apartment at The Cove did. It didn't feel like home because the people who made those places home weren't there anymore. She sat up and realized she had fallen asleep fully dressed, on top of her blankets with her phone still in her hand. She looked at it and saw a half-typed text message to Nikki. Some inane, half asleep missive about how Orville Redenbacher was the Colonel Sanders of Indiana. The time stamp on the text read three in the morning.

She looked at the clock on her nightstand and saw it was 08:00. Five hours of rough sleep wasn't great, but it was better than nothing. After a couple cups of coffee and a hot shower she'd be fine. Paige stretched once more then got up and told Kiku to start the coffee.

Paige didn't call Monarch like she said she would. She never had any intention of it. There was no reason she couldn't work her shift and catch up with her schoolwork after. Besides, it wasn't like Alpha would be around to check on her anyway. As far as Paige was concerned, what Alpha didn't know wouldn't hurt either of them. After the aforementioned shower and coffee, Paige was feeling surprisingly functional.

That afternoon, Paige stood in the exam room at the SRC alternating her gaze between her tablet and the Jane who was sitting on the workbench in front of her. She read and reread the description of her patient's malfunction as though she expected it to change into something less ridiculous with each pass. After she read the description for the fifth time, Paige decided that, nope, that was that and it was not going to get any better. She sighed and looked up at the scrapper, tired and exasperated; her coffee hadn't exactly had the lasting effect she'd hoped. "So, just so we're clear," she began— she couldn't believe she was having this conversation, "just because synthetics can't be poisoned doesn't mean it's okay for you to drink paint." She noticed a faded green smear around her patient's mouth from where he wiped the paint from his face.

"I know we're not supposed to, but—"

"But what? What could have possibly convinced you this was a good idea, Private…" she looked at her tablet for a name, "Dabney?"

"Dabney?" she thought. That's the worst name yet, and it certainly

didn't match his appearance. Dabney looked like Fer. Or rather, Fer's red-headed cousin. In the almost two years she'd been at Fort Thomas, Paige had seen probably three dozen Fer cousins— including Mirth. Sometimes she thought about trying to round them all up for a group picture, but she knew that would be impossible, mostly because Fer would likely have something to say about it.

"What? You think it's funny these assholes all have my face?" Because of course *he* wouldn't have *their* faces. *"Yeah, yeah, I came off an assembly line. Laugh it up. Not all of us get to be pretty custom jobs like Nix."* Never mind nobody knew a thing about Nix, not even Nix himself. For all anyone knew there could be a hundred Nix-like synthetics running around New York right this minute walking dogs or driving taxis.

Paige had to stop herself from diving down yet another rabbit hole, this time one in which Nix was behind the wheel of a taxi saying things like, "Where to?" or "What, no tip?" in a gruff New York accent. She blinked a few times and remembered the dumbass sitting on her work bench. "Well?" she asked him. "Are you going to explain how this happened, or are you just going to sit there?"

"It was… well… I…" Private Dabney floundered for an excuse to justify his actions and found none. "Look, it was a dare, okay? A couple guys in my platoon dared me to. My taste receptors are completely busted, so I can eat basically anything. Yesterday, I ate about a dozen ghost peppers. The day before, it was an entire jar of straight vegemite."

"Vegemite?" Where the hell did he get a jar of vegemite?

"Yeah, it's an Australian thing. You put it on toast."

"I know what vegemite is, Private."

"Oh. Well, you just seemed confused there for a second."

"Oh, I'm confused alright. I'm confused as to how your shenanigans escalated from, you know, food products, to shit you get at the hardware store. I mean, what the hell? Also, hooray! There's food in there too, so now the paint's going to be a sludge."

"Yeah, but—"

"Please stop talking before you tell me you also ate a wheel of cheese or—"

"It was a 20-inch anchovy and sauerkraut pizza."

Paige squeezed her eyes shut and regretted not staying home. "Of course it was." She chewed on her lips and shook her head in a slow, why-is-this-happening-to-me kind of way. "Why does gaining sentience always result in an immediate loss of common sense?" she groaned.

"Hey, I'm not here for you to get pissy with me. I'm here to—"

Paige perked up at Dabney's own apparent pissiness and cut him off. "You're here to get your guts cleaned out before that paint jams your systems, and Oompa Loompas have to drag your seizing, overheating ass out of here, singing about what an idiot you are," she said with all the bedside manner of a prison warden.

Paige picked up a scanning device with a small screen on it and aimed it at Dabney's midsection, examining the mass stewing in his digestive system. Behind her, Virgil, who was there to oversee the procedure, tried to curb his young coworker's attitude. "Come on, Paige, ease up. It is kind of funny. We'll clean him out and he'll be fine."

Paige didn't reply, she just gave an annoyed grunt. When she was satisfied with the information on the scanner, she put it down and approached the tool chest in the far corner of the room. "So, who put you up to all these dares?" she asked as she selected her tools from the chest. "I'll see to it they're written up."

Dabney shook his head. "No, it's fine. I don't want to get anyone in trouble."

"And I don't want you back in here next week because they dared you to chug lighter fluid, and you're too stupid to say no."

"Hey, Paige, I don't think that's necessary. Why don't you step outside until I get things set up here? You seem a little agitated," Virgil said as he assembled the suction pump.

"A little?!" Dabney scoffed. "If this is a little agitated, I'd hate to see her a lot agitated."

Paige glared at him; stone faced. "Oh, you're about to see me a lot agitated if you don't give me the information I want. So, you can tell me who did it on your own, or I'll just pull the memory files myself while you're sedated."

Dabney's eyes bugged like he'd just watched her shoot cats for fun. Virgil noticed this and was likewise having a similar reaction. He wasn't sure what caused Paige to come in and basically rototill the whole procedure, but it needed to stop before she got them in trouble.

"What Paige means," Virgil explained, trying to save face. "Is that she has never and will never violate our code of ethics because that is immoral and wrong." He stared daggers into her as he said those last few words.

"But she just said—" Dabney began.

"She's joking." More daggers were sent in Paige's direction.

Paige saw the glares and caught them readily. "The hell I am!" she snapped, taking the tube from Virgil.

"Oh, no. Nope. I don't think I want you working on me," Dabney said and hopped off the workbench.

"Private Dabney, I assure you, Paige is one of our best repair techs," Virgil reassured him.

"She's an arrogant kid who thinks she's smarter than me!"

"I am smarter than you, Private Paint-Drinker!" She shook the long rubber hose at Dabney as Virgil dragged her out of the exam room by her arm.

"What on earth has gotten into you?" Virgil demanded as they stood in the empty hall just outside Dabney's exam room. "You can't treat patients like that! Do you realize just how many codes of ethics you've violated just by threatening to access his memory against his will? Do you?"

"Do *you*?" Paige replied, unthreatened by Virgil's anger.

"I know it's enough that, for your sake, you should probably stop acting like a complete horse's ass in there! Yeah, the guy's an idiot, but that's his problem, not ours. We're here to fix scrappers, not berate and violate them!"

Paige rolled her eyes and crossed her arms. She looked every bit the sulky teenager she was. "Fine. Sorry."

"No. Not fine. I want you to go home for the rest of the day. Relax, calm down, clear your head. You seem like you need it."

"Oh, come on, Virgil!" Paige objected. "Look, I get it, I lost my temper. But I'm fine. I don't need to go home."

"You're not fine, Paige. And I'm not going to let you work on Private Dabney or anyone else today for that matter. Now, why don't you just head on home before I decide to get Monarch involved."

Paige looked at Virgil equally enraged and hurt. She was fine. Why didn't he understand that? Besides, Dabney the dumbass in there deserved everything he got. What kind of fuck for brains drinks paint on a dare and then refuses to out the guys who put him up to it? Goddamn it, he'd probably be right back in there next week because those same assholes put him up to something else.

"I—" she began but Virgil shook his head.

"Go home, Paige."

She pursed her lips and her face puckered up. She was trying to look angry and defiant but was coming across more like she'd just taken a spoonful of lemon juice. "Fine," she said. "Have fun cleaning all the garbage out of his system."

How? How could Virgil be siding with that fucking idiot? she thought as she walked back to Alpha's hou— er… home… as she walked back home. That scrapper needed a good verbal ass kicking, maybe even a literal one, too. Anyone who drinks paint and eats garbage just because his buddies dare him to, needs some sense knocked into him. She shook her head and rounded the corner and could see Alpha's house— shit… her house— just down the way. She watched its tidy front lawn with its winding sidewalk and elegant lamp post draw nearer with each step. Her house. She was never going to get used to that.

Just wait and see, she continued from her imaginary soap box. *"Dabney the Dumbass will be back. He'll be back, and I'll be the only one who isn't surprised."*

She got up to her room and asked Kiku if there were any new messages for her. The chipper little AI confirmed there were none, but did let her know Alpha would be late getting in. When Paige asked if that was a good or bad thing, Kiku told her she didn't understand the question.

Shaking her head, Paige changed into a pair of fuzzy pajama pants and an oversized sweatshirt. She opened her laptop, re-started the video she had been watching the previous night, and used her other computer to open the first of her late homework assignments. She needed to write an essay about that stupid 2029 pandemic.

Her mind flashed back to Mr. Larson's class. She saw Nikki glaring at her, and the whispers of the class after she lost her temper rang in her ears. She stared at the blank screen in front of her and shook her head. Nope. No dice. Skip this one.

The next assignment was calculus. She worked her way through the first equation while the internet star on the other computer comically screamed and cursed at the game he was playing. She glanced over at the stream just in time to see a fist coming straight at the screen, beginning what appeared to be a boss fight.

She blinked and saw Master Park's Studio and Fer's fist coming toward her. It was like her brain was a playlist set to random. The guy on the computer screamed and even though it was just for comedic effect, Paige felt every muscle in her body tense. The playlist shuffled. Her scar began to hurt even though nothing had touched it. The guy on the computer screamed again. Jesus Christ, was screaming like a buffoon all this guy could do? The list shuffled once more, and she wondered where Fer was right now and how he and the others were faring on their mission.

Shuffle.

She thought about the SRC and wondered if Virgil was going to tell Monarch about what happened with Private Dabney. Could she get fired over something like that? Surely not. Right?

Shuffle.

She needed to do her calculus. And her essay. And read two chapters for her chemistry class. But why? Why was any of that important?

Shuffle.

"Jesus Christ, why is that guy still screaming at a goddamned video game?"

Paige reached out and slammed the laptop closed so hard, that for a second, she thought she might have broken it. She sat there at her desk staring, now transfixed at the little picture disc that was behind the computer. It was one of those souvenir photo displays she got at an amusement park on one of her family's rare vacations. The slim, round base projected a slow-motion image of the Bryan family in a roller coaster car plummeting down the track. Paige and her mom were side by side in the front of the car, screaming in delighted terror with their arms raised above their heads, riding the coaster, the way a cowboy would a bull in a rodeo. Behind them, her dad looked about five seconds away from passing out, clutching his harness for dear life.

Paige watched the image play, then replay, over and over. It was from the summer before they moved. She closed her eyes and pictured the amusement park. Her dad, stopping to pose and get a picture with every costumed mascot they passed. The smell of the funnel cakes and pizza. The roar of the roller coasters. Her mom teasing her dad about his fear of fast-moving rides. Dad always did prefer the steady predictability of the carousel to the reckless abandon of roller coasters, or even the tilt-a-whirl.

Paige opened her filing cabinets and tried to find that specific memory and pull it out. She heard her mom's laughter and realized then she rarely ever heard her mom laugh, like really laugh. She was always so buried in her work, and when she did, it was always more of a sarcastic snort than an actual laugh. That day, she laughed. She laughed for real and, in Paige's memory, it sounded sweeter than all the symphonies in the entire world.

She recalled the way her legs dangled below her as she zoomed through the air on the coasters, and the big, dorky grin her dad had on his face when he won a little gray and white stuffed cat at one of the game booths. It was hardly an impressive win, and it had cost him far more than the little wad of cloth and fluff was worth. But Paige remembered the look of accomplishment and pride on his face when he gave it to her, and she knew, to her dad, that little cat was worth every penny. When he asked what she was going to name it, Paige just blurted out the first name that came to mind. "Kevin," she told him. "His name is Kevin." And Kevin it was.

The image of the roller coaster made another loop and this time Paige found she was crying as she watched the image go by. There would never be any more days like that. She'd never hear her mom laugh again or even be angry for that matter. She'd never get to pick on her dad for being shamelessly uncool. And she'd never get to hear him quote Tolkien or Bradbury anymore.

This sudden realization, this finality, struck Paige with such dread; she closed her eyes and forced herself to keep those memories. She pictured herself saving the data and copying it over and over to make sure there would be no possible way she would ever forget those insignificant, stupid, beautiful things; those things that hurt so much now that they were gone.

She opened her eyes again and saw her calculus in front of her and knew there was no way she'd ever get her work done. How could she be expected to do homework? And what was the point anyway? She got up and crossed the room to her bed where she grabbed a tissue from the box on her nightstand. She wiped her eyes and blew her nose but didn't feel any better.

From behind her, Kiku announced the time and asked if Paige would like her to order dinner. Paige knew she should eat but nothing sounded good. Instead, she curled up on her bed, tucking Kevin into the crook of one arm, and with fresh tears streaming down her face, tried to go back to the amusement park.

The line for the roller coaster stretched for miles in either direction. Paige leaned out of the queue and craned her neck, looking up and down the line, panicked. She had to get home, but the only way home was the ride, and the line wasn't moving. Why wasn't the line moving? She had to go home. Didn't they realize she was late?

She was late?

Late for what?

She didn't know, and it didn't matter. She was late and her parents were waiting on her. Goddamn this stupid slow line.

She had to go. She pushed her way forward through the river of strangers with a heavy slowness that felt like she was waist deep in molasses. The strangers didn't object to this, but they didn't clear a path for her either.

"Move! I have to get through! I'm late, and Mom's going to be pissed!" She looked up at the strangers; they were so tall. So tall she couldn't even see their faces. It was like everything above their chests was lost in a haze of clouds, like mountain peaks.

She made her way to the front of the line and found herself standing on the ride's loading platform, but instead of a roller coaster train, she saw a black sedan. She approached the car and tapped on the tinted driver's side window. It lowered with a soft hum, and she saw Nix.

"I need to get home; can you give me a ride?" she asked.

Nix didn't look at her; he just kept staring straight ahead with his face obscured in shadow. "I'm sorry Paige, I have to go. They need me at Fort Shelley." His voice was flat and void of any emotion.

"But I have to get home! I'm late! Mom's going to be mad if she has to wait on me! She's scared, and I need to get home and let her know I'm okay!" she begged, tears rolling down her cheeks.

"Your parents aren't home. They're at the mall. I saw them there myself."

"Then take me there! I have to find them!"

She watched Nix turn his head to look at her still unable to see his face. "I'm sorry, Paige. I have to go." Paige froze. Where was his face? Why was there nothing but a shadow there? And why wasn't he calling her Miss Bryan? Nix never called her by her first name. "I'm sorry, Paige. I have to go," he said again, and the darkened window slid back up.

"No! No! Nix!" she shouted as she watched the sedan drive down the track and out of sight.

Paige stood on the empty platform and stared at the spot where the car had been parked. The track was gone and there was a dark abyss in its place. From behind her, someone shouted, "Hey, you're holding up the line! Get moving!"

Get moving? Get moving into what? There was nothing there. If she stepped off the platform she'd fall and kill herself. "Get moving!" the voice barked at her again, and this time she felt hands pushing her from behind toward the edge of the platform.

"What are you doing? There's nothing there! Stop it!" she protested as they pushed her closer and closer to the edge.

"You're holding up the line! You cut all the way up here and now you're holding us up! Get moving!"

"But there's nothing—" Paige felt the platform floor vanish beneath her with one last push from the angry mob, and she plummeted into the blackness below.

Paige's eyes fluttered open with a gasp as she jolted awake, bathed in a cold layer of sweat. Her heart was pounding, and when she saw nothing but darkness, she feared she was still falling. She made herself blink a few times, and once her eyes adjusted, she realized she wasn't lost in the void, she was just lost.

Her already racing heart sped up when she realized she wasn't in her bedroom, or at least not her bedroom as she knew it. Where was she? How did she get there? It didn't matter. She still needed to get home. She looked around the room and saw her backpack. Again, she wondered how she wound up in this strange room, and hoped she wasn't far from her apartment. Mom was going to be so pissed.

Paige crossed the bedroom and grabbed the backpack. She looked around the room to try and find her shoes but didn't see them. She'd have to go home barefoot and buy new shoes later. She made one last attempt to find some shoes but instead saw Kevin sitting on the bed. She scooped him up knowing her dad's feelings would be hurt if she left him behind. He was older though, and rattier than when her dad gave him to her. It had only been a few hours. She must have dropped him at the park and messed him up or something.

She peered out the bedroom door and saw a long hallway leading to a stairway looking

out over a living room below. It was dark. Whoever was keeping her there must have been gone or asleep or something. Her bare feet were almost inaudible as they fell against the smooth wood floor. When she got to the stairs, she could see a foyer just to the right, beyond the living room, and made her way toward it. She reached the foyer and grabbed the door handle and pulled. It was locked. She pulled at the handle again, rattling the door in its frame, then heard a voice from the small glowing screen on the wall nearby. She stared at the screen, trying to make sense of it, when it spoke again.

"Do you want me to unlock the door, Paige?"

Paige jumped. The voice wasn't angry like the people on the platform or indifferent like Nix. This voice was feminine and friendly. She looked at the screen, confused.

"Would you like me to unlock the door?" the voice asked again.

Paige didn't know who this computer lady was, or how she knew her, and she didn't care. She was offering to unlock the door for her, so she couldn't be that bad. Paige looked at the luminous blue and green screen and said, "Yes." Her voice was clipped and nervous. "Yes, I need to get home. I'm late and—"

Click

The lock released, and without another word, Paige was out the front door sprinting across the cool, dewy lawn.

*

Alpha was happy to be headed home for the night, or what was left of it anyway. He glanced at the time display on his HUD and saw it was just after one in the morning. He refocused his gaze to the windshield of the car which was lit up in a soft blue glow similar to his HUD, showing the time, the speed at which he was traveling, and any traffic warnings that may be of concern to him. The time on the windshield display, he confirmed, also read just after one.

Fer's team had arrived back at Fort Thomas just after nine, successful in their mission and with a renewed and even better relationship with their Texan allies. After they were all debriefed, they had the not-so-easy task of processing the refugees. The processing itself wasn't difficult, it was just this time there were so many. The ones who needed medical help were taken to the SRC where they were fixed and cleaned up. The others were sent to the base's temporary housing facility where they too would be given the opportunity to clean up, recharge, and slowly begin the transition into Eastern US society.

"I hope we have enough room," Alpha thought to himself then decided, if there wasn't, he'd just have to utilize some of the empty apartments on the premises for the overflow. The reports from the Fort Isaac scout drones hadn't sent back wholly accurate hostage numbers. Well, better extra hostages than extra resistance. He reclined in his seat a little, relieved to have his scrappers home and proud of the work they accomplished today.

The car rounded the corner. Up the road, Alpha saw something had activated the motion lights in the front yard. Then, he noticed a figure rushing across the lawn. He leaned forward and zoomed in to see Paige, barefoot, in her pajamas, taking off down the street. She had her backpack on and Kevin in the crook of her arm. The car's headlights hit her, and she raised her other arm to block the sudden light before she took off running. "Kiku, pull over," Alpha ordered, and the car obeyed.

He got out just in time to intercept Paige as she passed the car. He stepped into her path with his arms out to either side, blocking her way. "Paige, it's late, what's going on? Why aren't you home, and where are your shoes?"

"I can't find my shoes," she said, not looking at him but rather beyond him. Alpha tried to step into her line of sight. There was something wrong with her. Her voice, there was something not right about it. It was disconnected and tense, like her brain was operating on overdrive.

"Well, let's go home and look for them. It's still cold out, you can't be barefoot out here," he told her, still trying to assess the situation.

"Yeah, I've got to get home."

Alpha nodded and tried to usher her to the car, but she jumped back and tried to make her way further down the sidewalk. "I have to go home! I'm late! Mom's been waiting, and she's scared, and I missed the roller coaster."

"Roller coaster?" It was then Alpha realized the distant, out-of-touch look on Paige's face was because she had no idea where she was or what was going on. Was she sleep walking or just having a bad dream? He couldn't say for certain, but he knew he had to snap her out of it. She wasn't thinking straight or perhaps not even at all. "Paige," he said, taking her by her shoulders. "You need to go home with me."

"But Mom—"

"Your mom..." he didn't want to say it. He couldn't do it the first time in the hospital room, and he knew he couldn't do it here. "Your mom," he began again, "You know where your mom is, Paige. You were there. So was I." He put a hand to her face. Her eyelashes were wet from crying. He felt tears on her cheek and wiped them away. "It's okay. It hurts me too, but you've got to wake up and come back. Come on, kiddo." He saw her blink three or four times, returning a little more to the here and now each time.

"They're gone," she whispered. Alpha watched the fog lift from her face and reality set in. "I was trying to go home. I wanted to go home." Her voice trembled and she held Kevin close. "I thought it was real, and I wanted to go home." Alpha watched as fresh tears welled up in her eyes and the sting of her loss hit again. "I want my parents. I want to go home."

Alpha stumbled backward a step as Paige threw herself into him, crying into his jacket lapels. "I know you do, kiddo," he replied, holding her, and giving her what comfort he could there under the streetlamp. "I know you do, and if I could find a way, I would do it; I would bring them back and send you home with them, but I can't." He felt Paige nod in understanding, and he took a step back. "I can't," he said again. The words fell heavy from his lips, and the weight they carried with them was of break-stomping finality. He continued, softer this time, "But what I can do is lead by their example and love you and worry about you and do my best to keep you safe and happy."

"You don't have to worry about me," Paige mumbled, wiping her eyes with her sleeve.

Alpha looked her up and down and couldn't help the smile on his face. "Paige, we're standing in the sidewalk in the middle of the night. You're in your pajamas and don't have any shoes on. I think I've got a right to worry."

Paige looked down at her bare feet and wiggled her sparkly purple toes. She observed her fuzzy pants and looked at Kevin, still in a death grip under her arm. Her head moved, it seemed, of its own accord as it made a path up and down, agreeing that Alpha's assessment of her was unfortunately spot on.

"Yeah," she said. "You're right. I've been... I've..." she sighed and no longer wanted to make excuses. "I'm worried about me, too."

"That's good," Alpha assured her. "It's okay that you're not okay. No one is expecting you to be after what you've been through."

Paige nodded, and he ushered her over to the still running sedan. "It feels good to say it," she said, managing a smile, a tired one, but a smile all the same.

"It does. And tomorrow I'll call Dr. Shipley and we'll see about getting both of us a little extra help." He held the door open for her, and she got inside.

"I like that idea." Paige scooted over and Alpha climbed into the back seat beside her.

"Good," he smiled. "Now, let's go home."

Paige nestled against Alpha and let her head rest on his shoulder. It felt like her brain had been replaced by a worn-out car battery. "Yeah," she agreed, and closed her eyes as they made the short ride up the road. "Let's go home."

Girls' Night Out Part 2

The Raid

ANJIKO AND INO had been watching the small rental house for the better part of two hours from inside one of Section's unmarked cars. The sun was low on the horizon, and the street outside was bustling with traffic, mostly students from the nearby university, all out to kick off a weekend of partying.

"What exactly are we looking for, Ino?" Anjiko, who had been watching the passersby with unabashed envy, asked from the passenger seat.

"We are assessing the situation," Ino replied, not taking her eyes from her phone.

"That drone's been out there for-ev-er. It's a house party not a hostage situation. There aren't even any armed guards, just a yappy dog."

"A guard dog."

"It's smaller than a cat! What's it going to do? Annoy us to death?"

Ino snapped her attention from the screen and glared at Anjiko. "I'm sorry, but you seem to have forgotten who we're dealing with. This man is a monster! A psychopath who doesn't care who he hurts as long as he gets what he wants!" She turned back to the phone. "We do this right, or we don't do it at all."

Anjiko watched her friend study the drone footage and slumped down in her seat with a groan. "Worst girls' night ever."

She was about to go back to staring out the window and daydreaming about the margarita which was now becoming less and less of a possibility, when Ino looked up and slipped her phone into her jacket pocket.

"Let's go," she said, opening the door.

Anjiko perked up. "Finally!"

They made their way up the street making sure to stay as inconspicuous as possible and stopped in front of the small rental house to survey it from the sidewalk. "So, how heavy do you think that door is?" Anjiko asked.

"On a rental unit like this?" Ino's eyes lit up, and she scanned the door. "Seventy-one pounds. Why do you ask?" She looked over her shoulder and saw Anjiko pull a zip-top sandwich bag from the breast pocket of her jacket, the top of which was folded over and secured into place with a bright green yucky-face sticker. Inside the bag was a small block of what looked like modeling clay. "What is that?"

The two ducked behind a giant maple tree on the edge of the lawn to stay out of sight.

"My lucky C-4," Anjiko replied. Ino just stared. "What? Too much?"

"Yes, too much. Why do you have C-4 in your pocket anyway?"

"In case something needs blown up, duh."

"Well, it's not going to do you much good without a lucky detonator to go with it."

Anjiko reached into one of the cargo pockets on her pants and pulled out a small remote control. "You mean this?"

"We are not blowing anything up. Put that back and just follow my lead," Ino said as they ascended the rickety front porch steps.

Outside the door, they heard the low thump of bass from the music playing inside. Anjiko looked to her left then right and saw the blinds on one of the front windows move. A second later, a tiny Pomeranian poked its head through the slats.

"Um, Ino," Anjiko said as she watched the dog bare its teeth at them. "I think our cover's about to be blown."

They both watched, stunned as the little dog let out a machine-gun burst of sharp barking.

"I told you it was a guard dog!" Ino snapped. "Come on, let's get to work!"

"Then, margaritas," Anjiko assured herself and took her position behind Ino. "So are you going to knock or...." She watched Ino hike up her knee and thrust her foot forward into the door with a crash. "Oor we're kicking the door in. Okay, that also works."

The door swung fast and wide, almost a blur, its hinges hanging onto the frame for dear life. There was a sharp crack from the doorknob as it broke through the drywall, where it stuck fast.

"Work time, Anjiko!" Ino barked.

Anjiko pushed forward, shouting, "Scrappers! Don't move!"

A scream came from the sofa to their left, and they saw a young woman curled up in a ball, holding a throw pillow in front of herself like a shield. Beside her, her friend jumped to her feet, spilling a plastic cup of beer all over the coffee table. Further across the way, a group of people in the kitchen stood frozen over a stack of pizza boxes, staring speechless at the scrappers. Somewhere in the house, someone killed the music, leaving nothing but the incessant yapping of the Pomeranian and stunned gasps of the humans.

Ino and Anjiko surveyed the room.

"Where is—" Ino began, but a cough cut her short. Pungent smoke hung thick in the air. "Where is—"

"Where's the skunk with the dirty gym socks?" Anjiko asked, waving the smoke out of her face. "Jeeze."

"What the hell is going on?" a dark-haired woman demanded, storming out of one of the side rooms. "We didn't call scrappers! There aren't even any synths in this house!" She looked at the door and the hole it had put in the wall. "Are you fucking kidding me? There goes my security deposit! And you better believe you're going to pay for that!" She rushed to the still barking dog and scooped it up in her arms where it continued to bark and snarl at them. "You ever heard of knocking!"

"Yeah, I suggested that, too," Anjiko said.

"Jesus Christ, you can't just kick someone's door in! I don't care what part of the government you're with! We have rights, you know, and you better believe I'll be taking this up with... well... whoever I take this up with!"

Anjiko watched the woman and the dog as they continued to yell and bark respectively, and tried to pay attention, but the people in the room directly to her right were playing the latest updated version of Werewolf Hollow, and the little girl in her head really wanted to play too.

"Hey! I'm talking to you!" the angry lady snapped. "You can't just kick my door in!"

Anjiko glanced down at her and back to the TV, the yelling having turned into white noise some thirty seconds back. "Yeah, no. Totally," she said, not even half aware of what the woman was saying and motioned toward Ino. "Talk to her, she's in charge."

"We're looking for Vincent May. Where is he?" Ino didn't give the lady a chance to be snippy with her.

"Vince? What the hell do you want with Vince?"

"That's classified. Where is he?"

The implication that her housemate might be in government-level trouble seemed to cool the woman's temper considerably, and the next time she spoke there was more worry than anger in her voice.

"Did he do something wrong? Are you going to arrest him? He's not even synthetic!"

"I will ask you again, Ma'am. Is he here?"

Every set of eyes in the room were on the young woman and her finally silent dog, waiting for her answer.

"He left to get more beer," she said.

"He did?" Ino watched the woman's expression grow more anxious.

"W-what are you doing?" she asked when she saw the light in Ino's optics intensify. "What's wrong with your eyes?"

"You're lying," Ino said, and watched the color drain from the woman's face.

There was the sound of rapid footfalls from somewhere down the hall and a second later, Vincent May tore through the kitchen. He stopped just long enough to let out a distressed, "Oh shit!" at the sight of the scrappers before he bolted out the back door.

"That's him!" Ino shouted and turned to Anjiko but found she was nowhere to be seen. "Anjiko! Anjiko, where are you!" She looked around and spied her counterpart in the side room with four other people, controller in hand, cheering at the TV as she gleefully tore through a forest of murderous werewolves. "Anjiko! What are you doing?" She looked around the room; the smoke was thickest in here, and the humans inside were all kicked back on an assortment of recliners, eating pizza as they played.

Anjiko looked up from the TV and saw Ino glaring at her.

"Did you find him?" she asked.

Ino's hand clamped over her arm, and she dragged her to her feet. "Yes! And he's fled the scene," she said. "Let's go!"

"Aaw, do we gotta? We were having fun." Anjiko looked down and saw the hellfire on Ino's face and sighed. "Fine." She looked at the random assortment of people in the room with her. "Sorry, everyone. Duty calls."

Anjiko was dragged from the room to a chorus of protests, all telling her to come back and hang with them and accusing Ino of being a buzzkill.

"Hurry up. He went out the back door," Ino said, ignoring the jeers coming from the game room.

"Man, why'd he have to run? I hate it when they run," Anjiko complained, then stopped halfway through the kitchen in front of a row of large pizzas. "Ooh, snacks." She reached out and grabbed a slice of pepperoni.

"Focus, Anjiko," Ino reminded her, taking the pizza from her hand, and putting it back in the box. "He's already gotten too far ahead of us."

"Fine, fine, I'll focus," she grumbled as she followed Ino out the back door and across the yard. "But you're buying the margaritas now."

Family Night

Fer

IF I HAD a heart, it would be fucking pounding right now, but I don't. My senses, however, are on high alert as Melissa and I walk toward the restaurant. It's about 20:00 on a Saturday, and it's a beautiful spring night. You couldn't ask for nicer. Clear skies, a warm breeze, blooming trees. Yeah. It's pretty gorgeous. Too bad I can't enjoy it, what with the massive panic attack I'm about to have. I can spot all the passing glances and register the shifts in the temperature outside. I don't want to, but I'm nervous, and when I'm nervous I notice everything. Right now, specifically, I'm noticing I'm sweating my ass off in my dress uniform despite it not even being that hot out. What can I say? Everything in me is on overdrive, and I'm running hotter than normal as a result. I activate my internal cooling system and start to feel a little better. Of all the things I've done in my life, all the missions I've been on, all the corruptions I've put down, this will be the death of me. I fucking know it.

We stop in front of a small Korean restaurant on 4th street and sit down at one of the outdoor tables. My HUD says it's 19:55. We're early, but just a little. A server comes over and I put in a drink order. I can't get drunk, but it has a nice placebo effect. Melissa does the same. She's just as nervous as I am. I can tell. She hasn't stopped fidgeting with her necklace since I picked her up. As we wait, I continue to take in the people around us. Most of them don't pay us any attention. A few give my uniform the once over then go on about their business like the good little monkeys they are. Granted, Melissa and I rarely have issues going out together. Every now and then, someone will hassle us, but once they realize we both can kick their ass six ways from Sunday, they back down. I stop surveying the patio when I hear her give a nervous sigh.

"We don't have to do this," I tell her and take her hand from across the table.

"No, we do. We should. I want you to meet my family. I want you to be part of my family."

"That's all well and good, but…" I trail off trying to decide how to breach the subject.

"What exactly have you told them about me?"

"I told them you work for Section, you're a scrapper, and that you were one of my students."

"Did you tell them I'm synthetic?"

Melissa looks away and frowns. "I told them you're the Omega Squad Captain; that sort of makes it pretty obvious without outright saying it, right? I mean, they like synthetics well enough. It's just…"

"They won't like one dating their daughter?" I'm not mad, I know this kind of thing can be hard to do alone, just a little annoyed. "Melissa—" The server cuts me off as he returns with our drinks. She picks hers up, it's a sort of blue, fruity cocktail, and takes a long pull from the straw, halfway draining the glass. I down my whiskey in one go and hail the server for another before he even exits the patio. "Melissa," I say again. "You should have told them. It's not fair to spring it on them like this."

"Spring what on us?" I hear an unfamiliar male voice behind me and bristle. Here we go. I look at Melissa. She smiles at me, and we stand up together.

"Mom, Dad," she begins, "I'd like you to meet Fer."

I turn around and face her parents. They're a typical looking couple, dressed for a nice night out. Mrs. Park is wearing bright red lipstick and her gray and black hair is pulled back into a tight kind of twist on her head. Mr. Park is in slacks and a jacket, his right hand extended to me, waiting for me to shake it. I do, and for a split second they're smiling. Then, his grip changes at the feel of my almost-human-but-not-quite skyn. He zeros in on my face, focusing on my eyes, and he realizes what I am. Or to be more accurate, what I'm not.

"You've got to be joking," he says, and drops my hand like it just burst into flames. Yep, we're off to a great start.

"Why would you say that?" Melissa asks. She's trying to sound casual, but I can hear the quiver in her voice, and feel the temperature change in her hand as she grips mine like a vise.

"Well, isn't it obvious?" Mrs. Park says, her voice shrill. "This can't be your boyfriend. He's— he's… well, look at him!"

"I know, I'm not what you expected," I say, trying to keep this train from derailing, but both her parents just glare at me like I slapped them right in the face. I look down at Melissa for a clue as to what to do next.

"How was your flight?" She tries to shift the conversation and offers them a seat at the patio table. Neither of them moves.

"How on earth could you be so inconsiderate?" her mother demands, and again, I try and keep things civil.

"Ma'am, neither of us have any intention of upsetting—"

"I mean, a synthetic?!" she continues like I'm not even fucking there. "How am I supposed to ever get grandchildren if you don't have the sense to settle down with someone who can…" she trails off and looks at me with contempt. Then she opens her purse and begins to dab her eyes with the tissue she pulls from it. Jesus guilt-tripping Christ.

The server has just returned with my next drink, and I slip a fifty-dollar bill onto his tray and tell him to just keep 'em coming. Again, I can't get drunk, but I'm sure as hell going to try.

"Mom, please, you're making a scene," Melissa glances at the staring passers-by as she pleads with her mother, who's making a big damn show of how emotionally devastated she is.

Hoo-boy are people staring. And talking. The Parks probably can't hear it, but I can. Most of them are just confused. Some want to step in and offer help. I hope they all just choose to mind their own damn business. One last time, I try to keep this powder keg from blowing.

"Let's just sit down, and I'm sure once we get to know each other—"

"No," Mr. Park snaps at me, and it takes all my resolve not to snap back. He shifts his venomous glare from me to Melissa. "We came all the way to Indiana to see you, and this is what you greet us with? I refuse to accept this as okay! It's not! I will not be okay with my daughter being one of those…"

I know where this is going. *"Don't say it,"* I think.

"Those..."

"Don't say it..."

"Dollies!"

He said it. He fucking said it. Everything inside me is on fire. I squeeze the glass in my hand so hard I can feel it starting to crack. I was prepared for them to be skeptical. I get it, your only kid being in a relationship with a someone who's not technically human is a bit unnerving. But they're more than unnerved. I can't fix this with a conversation over some kimchi jeon and drinks. My very existence in their daughter's life offends them on a fundamental level, and I don't know how I should react. I know how I *want* to react. I want to verbally disembowel Mr. Park for calling Melissa a dolly, and tell Mrs. Park that if her whole life revolves around coercing her daughter into giving her grandchildren, then she deserves to live forever with none. And...

"You're right, Dad. This isn't okay," I hear Melissa say. I look down and her fear and anxiety have given way to a staunch resolve. She picks up her drink and downs the rest of it. "I'm going to start this entire conversation over. This time, you can either behave like normal, reasonable people, and we can have some drinks, order dinner, and get to know Fer, or you can go back to your hotel. Hell, you can go back to the Coastal Union if our relationship is so terrible to you. It's your choice. But I'm proud of us." She pauses and waits for a response, but none ever comes. They just stand there in offended silence. "I love us, and what we have." She puts her arm around me and pulls me close. "And he does, too."

I stand there, speechless. No one has ever stood up for me like she just has. I know it sounds crazy; me, of all people, needing something like that, but it's true. It makes me feel good. It makes me feel wanted in a way I haven't felt since I was with Rho.

I look down at her. She's smiling. I want to kiss her, but I figure, given the current situation, it's probably not the best idea. Instead, I just reply, "Yeah...I love us, too." I hold her close and look at her parents who are breathing so hard they're starting to look like pufferfish. "Look, I know I'm not what you expected. I'm sorry. But... and they're leaving." I look down at Melissa. She has tears in her eyes as she watches her parents go.

They don't look back as they hail a ride and vanish down the street. After a minute, I lead her back to our table and we sit.

"I'm so sorry," I say. And I am. I truly am. The last thing I ever want to do is hurt Melissa or see her hurt.

"No," she sniffles. "I'm sorry. You shouldn't have to put up with this kind of treatment."

"And neither should you," I counter, and wipe the tears from her eyes. We're in this together, right?"

She smiles and nods. "Right."

"You still feeling up for dinner?"

She shakes her head and sucks up the final drops of her cocktail. "In all seriousness, I just want to go. I need some alone time."

I know when Melissa says she needs alone time, it usually means she's going to her martial arts studio to put the hurt on the heavy bag.

"Okay. I think that's a good idea. We both probably need to blow off steam. I'll probably head to Jet's for a bit."

I drop her off at her apartment, kiss her goodbye, and make my way to Jet's place feeling... off. I'm worried this night is going to stick around for a while. While Melissa handled it like the badass she is, I know parental approval is a huge thing for humans. I'm afraid this is going to eat at her. I'm afraid she's going to start second guessing us. I'm afraid I'm about to hit that fucking kid crossing the street. Wait... what?

I slam on my breaks and roll down my window, "Hey!" I snap. Then I realize I recognize this dumbass. "Monkey?"

*

Paige

I'm sitting on an uncomfortable folding chair inside an old factory. Okay, well, it used to be a factory. These days it's an event hall, and today, specifically, it's where my Junior Prom is taking place. Like, right now. As we speak. There are balloons, banners, and fancy holographic projectors that make the ceiling look like a starry night sky complete with aurora borealis. I'm not sure where this prom is supposed to take place because Bloomington sure as shit doesn't get many auroras, but, whatever, I guess it is kind of neat looking. In the middle of the ceiling, the disco ball dapples me and everyone else around me with little circles of light, and the DJ is playing a bass-heavy dance mix.

My phone vibrates on the table in front of me, and I see it's a text from Nix. He likes to keep in touch with me and Alpha from the Confederated Zone when he can, and I am 3000% okay with that. What? So, it's prom. Look, I could be on fire and I would still answer Nix's texts. This one is a picture of him holding a copy of *The Hobbit* with the words, *"Look what I'm reading,"* accompanying it.

"No fucking way," I type. *"Did you lose a bet?"*

A few seconds later, he texts back, *"No. A friend of mine loaned it to me."*

I am about to ask him if this is his way of signaling he is under duress and needs help because, well, Nix doesn't read books. But before I can, some jack-off bumps into the table and knocks over two of the half a dozen cups of punch sitting nearby. I jump out of my seat and flee the scene before my dress gets ruined.

I try to find the dumbass who bumped the table so I can tell him to watch what he's doing, but he's long gone, lost in the crowd of people dancing. On the edge of the dancefloor, I can see Nikki dancing with a few of the girls from her programming club. None of us have dates so we all decided to go to prom as a group. It's fine, I guess. Still, even as a group of friends, I feel like a fifth wheel. It's loud and crowded, and I am regretting this decision more and more with each passing minute.

I look down at my phone and realize I can't just leave Nix hanging, but my heart's no longer in it, so I just send back a GIF of Mr. Burns from *The Simpsons* drumming his fingers together saying, "Eeexcellent."

What was I thinking? I've barely been back in school for a full semester, and I still can't make it through a day without wanting to hide or cry or both. After Mom and Dad were killed and that whole bullshit custody battle was settled, I wound up moving in with Alpha. It's not a terrible arrangement. Alpha's house is swanky and bigger than our old apartment at The Cove. My room is twice the size of my old one, and I basically have everything I could ever ask for. Alpha's a great paper-dad; that's what I call him. Paper-Dad, as in Dad on Paper. He listens to me, gives me space when I need it, and likes watching old movies with me when I can't sleep. He gives me everything he possibly can. I have everything… except it's not the same.

It's been two years and I still think about them every day. Every. Day. At night I have dreams of the mall riots where I'm fighting through crowds that are like rivers of mud, and I can't move. Sometimes, I have dreams of running away from CPS agents who are trying to take me back to the Ellison's house. Every now and then I dream about Nix, though. Those are nice. Sometimes in those dreams we get all makey-outey and it's just the best. But then, I wake up and remember he's still over in the Confederated Zone... apparently reading *The Hobbit*. Also, he's not the least bit attracted to me. So, yeah, there's that.

Suffice it to say, despite Alpha's trying, the last two years have sucked. It's better than it was, but that doesn't mean it's great. I still don't sleep well, and most of the time I just want to lock myself in my room and be a lump. I know it's not what Mom or Dad would want, but I can't help it. I miss them, and it's my fault they're dead. No, I don't care what Alpha or my therapist says. It's my fault. I didn't get to them in time and... yeah.

Alpha took me out of school for my first semester this year. After the previous year of parent teacher meetings and my grades dropping like a lead box of rocks down an empty elevator shaft, he said we needed a break. So, twice a week for the last nine months we've both been meeting with a therapist; me to talk about and process what happened, and Alpha... shit... probably to vent about how much of a pain in the ass I am. Anyway, it's been helpful, I guess. Dr. Hohenstein, she's my therapist, got me on some meds and gave me all kinds of techniques for coping with my situation. It's been so helpful I told Alpha I felt up to going back to school. My grades are good, and I'm feeling like less of a lump. It's been going better than we expected, so a couple months ago, I told him I wanted to go to prom. And now, here I am, in my expensive dress with my hair a giant curled fire hazard thanks to the gallon of spray the stylist used, wanting to go home.

What? This is so dumb. Everyone's out there having fun like... well, like they're normal teenagers. Because they are. I'm... not. I don't know what I was expecting; probably some magical evening with a chance meeting that changes my perspective on life forever. You know, like in the movies, but this is not that.

I reach into my purse, a sparkly silver clutch that's more trouble than it's worth because it's a clutch and doesn't have a strap, hence the name, and pull out a little orange pill bottle. I pop one of my anxiety pills and swallow it with whatever the hell kind of punch they're serving up at the snack table. I know this will do nothing for my current situation. My meds don't work like that. They're not an immediate fix. I'm just hoping for a placebo effect that will maybe trick me into thinking I'm capable of a normal night with my friends.

"Hey wallflower, are you ever going to get up and dance?" I look up and see Nikki coming off the dancefloor toward me. She looks amazing in her bright red, skintight dress, rocking all her curves like a runway model. She's got a gigantic red hibiscus flower tucked behind her ear; it's so exotic, even though I know it just came from some florist. Her dress is bold, and her hair is this glorious natural heap of curls. I envy her. Like I said, my curls required two hours at the salon and hazardous amounts of chemicals. Please don't light any matches near me.

"I don't know if I'm up for dancing," I reply, and sip my punch. "You look like you're having fun with Emma, Chrissy, and everyone. I don't want to bring you guys down."

"You won't!" she argues. "I promise you won't!"

I stare into my cup like it's Galadriel's mirror and sigh. I don't dance. I've never danced. I don't even know if I know how to dance, and I'm not exactly sure tonight's the night to find out.

I look at her and see she's donned her best puppy dog face; her eyes are big and glossy, and her lower lip is jutted out. She looks pathetic and hilarious. "Come on. Please, please, please, pleeeease?" she whines.

I look back into my cup. I'd be lying if I said the last two years hadn't been hard on Nikki, too. I've been a pretty shitty friend for a while; bailing on her all the time and snapping at her because I don't know how to put my feelings into words. The least I can do is try and have fun.

"Okay, I'll go do the thing," I smile and find someplace safe to put my purse for the moment. As soon as it's stashed, Nikki grabs my hand and starts dragging me toward the dance floor. With each step the music seems to get louder and the room smaller. There are so many people out there. It's this massive sea of bodies all churning to the beat of the music and smells like about four dozen different kinds of perfumes and colognes all mixed together. I join the rest of our group and Chrissy says something to me, but I can't quite hear her over the music. I just give her a vague smile and try to pull everything I have on dancing from my filing cabinets, but nothing comes. The cabinets won't open. This isn't exactly new, but it freaks me out whenever it happens. My pulse quickens and I feel the blood rushing in my ears. Nikki nudges me with her elbow, and I make a few, stiff, dance-like movements. It's too crowded. I can't move. I'm sweating. I feel my palms go clammy and my face flush. The DJ drops the bass and I shrink. It's too loud and the constant spinning of the disco ball is nauseating.

"I have to go." I'm not sure how loud I said it or if anyone heard me. All I know is I said it and now I'm beating a path to the exit.

I slam into the crash bar and push the door open. I'm in the front parking lot. It's dark outside and so wonderfully cool. I gulp the air like I'm drowning and let the breeze cool me down a bit. I can still hear the music coming from inside, but it's not so loud and oppressive. I take a few more breaths when I hear the doors open behind me.

"Are you okay?" Nikki asks. "What happened?"

"I'm sorry, Nik," I reply. "I tried. I thought I could do it, but I can't. This was a bad idea. I'm so sorry. Please don't be mad at me. I'm sorry I'm still a fucking mess." I blink back the tears that are surfacing, because yes, let's panic *and* cry tonight. Go big or go home, right?

"Don't be sorry," Nikki says to me with a grin as she puts an arm around my shoulders. "I'm used to you being a mess by now." I manage to smile back, and my tears relent a bit. "Are you going home?"

"Yeah, I think so."

"Do you want me to drive you?"

I shake my head. There is no way I'm screwing up this night any further. "Nah, you stay. Have fun. There's a bus stop nearby. I'll catch a ride."

"Why don't you just call Alpha?"

"Because he'll try and convince me to stay, and I'm not up for that conversation right now."

"Are you sure you don't want me to drive you?" she asks again.

"I'm sure. A long, quiet bus ride will actually do me some good right now."

"Okay." Nikki lets me go but doesn't go back inside. "I'm sorry tonight sucked for you," she says. "But you made it out. That's a big step."

"I'm still a goddamned train wreck," I reply.

"Yeah, you are, but you're my goddamned train wreck, and I like you anyway." She gives me a big hug and makes me promise to text her when I get home. Then she goes back inside.

Once she's back at the dance, I make my way across the parking lot and down the sidewalk toward the bus stop. It's a clear twilight and the moon is bright and almost full. The streets are strangely empty for a Saturday night. Granted, I'm not on campus or near downtown where all the usual excitement is happening. I cross the street at the end of the block without looking and am engulfed in headlights. I freeze. Tires screech. A second later the headlights are pulled over at the curb.

"Hey!" someone yells at me. The bright lights switch off and I see Fer leaning out the window of his Jeep beneath the streetlamp. "Monkey?" He is not an unwelcome sight. Ever since Mom and Dad were killed, I've sort of understood Fer a bit better than I had before. Out of everyone—Alpha, Nikki, Master Park— Fer knows. I don't know how to say it any other way than Fer knows. He gets it. He gets me. And I get him now, too. We've both lost our families. We're both on the struggle bus. I'm actually kind of happy to see him. "Any particular reason you're roaming the streets at night dressed like a Disney Princess?" he asks.

"Nope. Just out here on a whim. Definitely not bailing on my prom after a panic attack," I lie with a casual shrug.

"Is that so?" He knows I'm lying just as well as I do.

"Yep. What are you doing out here?"

"Definitely not headed to Jet's after finding out Melissa's parents hate my shiny metal guts on the basis that I merely exist." He matches my initial reply, and ducks back into the Jeep. "See ya."

"Wait, wait, wait!" I say rushing toward the driver's side door as best as I can in these fucking heels. "I'm not going back to prom. I freaked out and bailed. I was going to catch a bus home." I rest my arms on the open window and smell the familiar cigarette smoke and suddenly I feel better. "Tonight's been a disaster," I admit. "Can I come with you to Jet's?" The adrenaline and panic from earlier have subsided, and I'm left starving with a raging headache.

I see Fer raise an eyebrow, the one with the scar, and he considers my request. His eyes are warm amber fires in the dark interior of the Jeep. Finally, after keeping me waiting just long enough to piss me off, he grins and unlocks the passenger door. "Get in, Monkey."

I climb in and buckle up. "Thank you," I say. The seat is comfortable. I feel like we're on our way home from one of our nights sparring at the Taekwondo studio. I feel normal. I feel like I don't have to pretend right now. We sit in silence for a block or so. I watch Fer pull a cigarette from his pocket and light it up. Much to my relief, my hair does not ignite into a massive fireball at the lighter's flame. Fer doesn't ask me any questions or pick on me as we drive through town. He knows better. He takes a long drag on his cigarette and exhales a dirty gray cloud that's immediately sucked out the open window.

"So, rough night?" I venture.

He smirks and gives a slow nod of agreement. "I met Melissa's parents tonight. I didn't want to. I told her it was a bad idea, but she insisted. Her parents only visit once every couple of years, and she figured it was time we met."

"And it went poorly?"

"Poorly is an understatement. There was crying, yelling, name calling, and it all ended with them leaving."

"Oh damn."

"Yeah. Oh damn, indeed."

"The first thing out of her dad's mouth when he saw me was, 'you've got to be joking.' They then went on to point out, in great length, how I am not, nor will I ever be, human. So, long story short, the three of them get into this argument outside the restaurant we're supposed to be having dinner at. Her mom's crying about how she'll never have grandbabies, like that's the end all be all of fucking human existence, and her dad's going on about how there's no way he's going to have a daughter who's a dolly."

I balk at the term. "He called her that?! Her own dad?!" I've been called a dolly plenty of times. I don't really care. It's a stupid term used by stupid people. But it's different to be called a dolly by people like Gwen and her lackies. I hate her guts, and she hates mine. She can call me a dolly and I can tell her to go fuck herself with a syphilitic pineapple. Now, if say, Nikki called me that, I think I'd probably die. "So, dare I ask how this all ended?"

"Melissa and I decided to leave the restaurant and just go our separate ways for the evening and let off some steam. So here I am. Off to let off steam."

The Jeep pulls into an open spot in front of The Olive Branch, or as we call it, Jet's, and we get out; the pathetic pair we are. We go inside and a big man in an apron greets us from behind the front counter. I like Jet. He's so nice and makes the best Stromboli in town.

Fer and I sit down at the bar. He doesn't even have to order. Shiraz, the server, just sits a glass of bourbon and Coke in front of him, and he thanks her. Jet is still staring at us like we've both grown extra limbs or are suddenly covered in polka dots. It's been a long time since I've been here.

"Soooo…What have you two been up to?" he asks. Fer just shakes his head and waves the question away; I guess he's reached his sharing limit today, so Jet turns to me for my response.

"Well, I had a panic attack and bailed on my prom. Fer met his girl-friend's parents, and it turns out they're synthophobic assholes."

"Hmm," he muses. "That explains the get-ups."

"Speaking of," Fer grunts and tugs his tie the rest of the way off, tossing it onto the counter. "That's better." He picks up his glass, drains it, and without even asking, Shiraz brings him another.

"Ooh, can I have what he's having?" I ask hopefully.

Jet leans across the counter toward me and gives me a big, warm smile. "Ask again in about four years."

I hang my head in defeat. "Well, it was worth a shot."

"You keep trying and I keep telling you no. I like you, Paige, but I'm not getting in trouble with the law for you."

"That's fair."

"But I'll be happy to get your usual going. I'll even get you a bib, so you don't get that pretty dress of yours dirty." He punches my order in on his tablet and sends it back to the kitchen.

"Yes to the food. No to the bib," I reply. I'm not a toddler.

"So, how have you been? It's been boring around here without you to diversify the clientele," Jet says. I look around, and as usual, I am the only human in the restaurant. But that's fine. I don't mind it and none of Jet's customers seem to mind me. In fact, I feel more comfortable here, around Janes, than I do around most other humans.

"Oh, you know, I've just been trying to get through the day," I reply.

"I do know. Is it getting better?"

"Well, I'm here, aren't I?" I smile and reach for my purse to pay for my meal. "Oh shit. I left my purse at the prom."

*

Alpha

I've been watching but not watching the TV for about two hours now, waiting on the edge of my seat for my phone to ring. Waiting for some disaster. Any minute now. Any minute.

This is hard; parenting, that is. It's especially hard when you're thrown in headfirst. Not to mention, the added bonus of your new daughter being plagued by all the trauma. I don't know what I'm doing. I've downloaded books I've watched lectures and TED talks online. I've even called Nikki's moms on occasion for advice. What must they think of me? One of the most influential people in the EUS military calling in the dead of night because Paige and I just spent the last hour screaming at each other, and now she's locked in her room sobbing. Apparently, that's normal teenage behavior. Who knew? Not me, that's for crap sure. The school problems, the mood swings, the nightmares… my gods, the nightmares. Granted, they've lessened as of late. Instead of two or three a week, we're down to two or three a month. Hooray for progress.

Actually, a lot of her difficult behavior has lessened, and not a moment too soon. So, when Paige approached me about wanting to go to prom a few months ago, I was ecstatic. It was the first time she wanted to socialize beyond her weekly martial arts classes since she moved in.

We went all out. She made a hair appointment, and I took her to try on dresses. The dresses proved to be a bit of a problem since most of them were either strapless or had spaghetti straps, and she was worried about people seeing her scars. Luckily, we were able to find a nice bolero for her to wear with her dress, and that helped. Everything seemed fine until tonight, just before Nikki arrived to pick her up, when she asked me if she still had to go. I told her it would do her good, but if things went badly, she could always call, and I'd come get her. So now, here I am, waiting for my cue.

I don't have to wait long. As soon as I finish my thought, Kiku announces an incoming call from Nikki. Aaand action.

"Is everything okay?" I answer without even greeting her.

"Oh, um, hi to you too, Alpha," she replies. "Are you okay? You sound tense."

"Sorry. Hello, Nikki. And I'm fine."

"That's good. I'm just calling to check and see if Paige got home. She left her phone at prom, and she said she'd text me when she got home."

I freeze. "What do you mean, Paige isn't at prom?"

"What do *you* mean, she's not at home?"

I'm on my feet now, pacing across the living room, my mind already playing out hundreds of scenarios all of which end badly. "Of course she's not at home. She's supposed to be with you at the prom. What happened?"

"Well, she sort of freaked out and had a panic attack. She got up to dance, made it to the floor for about five seconds, then noped her ass out the door like it was on fire. I followed her, and she said she was going to catch the bus home. And before you give me hell, I offered to drive her, but she turned me down. I told her to text me when she got home and when I didn't hear anything I called her cell, but she left her purse. So, I called the house." She pauses for a moment. "And you're telling me she's not home?"

"No." I say without thinking. "I mean, yes. I mean… she's not here. Do you have any idea if she might have gone somewhere else?"

Nikki pauses again, thinking. "Nothing comes to mind."

"Okay," I say. "I'm going to go look for her. Call my cell if she comes back to the dance."

"Screw that! Come pick me up. I'll search with you," she says, and I agree. I disconnect the call, put on some shoes, and bolt out the door. A few minutes later, I'm in the car riding to the dance hall. About twenty minutes later, I'm meeting Nikki in the parking lot.

"So, where do we start?" she asks as she climbs into the passenger seat and buckles up.

We circle the block hoping but not expecting her to still be nearby. Then we move on to the next block, and the next, until we reach Bryan Park (which is no relation to her or her family). Kiku parks the car, and we get out to search it. The park is small, so it doesn't take us long to realize she's not there.

"Do you think she would have gone on to campus?" I ask, looking in the direction of nearby Indiana University. "It's just a couple blocks away."

"No. I doubt it."

"That's good," I say with a relieved sigh. The IU campus is huge and having to find Paige on it would be a nightmare. "Should we try the next block over?"

"I think we should start working a bit smarter," Nikki replies. "She said she was going to take a bus. Let's assume she did. Where are some places on the bus route she might go to instead?"

I open a map of the city bus routes on my HUD and highlight the one Paige would most likely be on. I go stop by stop until I see it. "Master Park's Studio is on the city bus route," I say. "And if Paige is upset, she'll probably want to hit something."

"That is a solid truth," Nikki agrees, and we take off for Park Taekwondo.

When we pull up to the building, we see the lights are on and there's someone inside. I breathe a sigh of relief, but then I see the figure through the front window. It's not Paige. I start to feel tense again.

We enter the studio and see Melissa Park vigorously assaulting a large canvas punching bag in the far corner of the studio. The bag swings and the chains squeal each time she lands a hit. She doesn't even realize we're here.

"Excuse me, Master Park?" Nikki calls across the room.

The small woman at the bag throws one more kick, then turns around. "Alpha, Nikki," she greets us. For a split second, she's smiling. Then she sees my face which probably looks like I've just ridden a dozen roller coasters with a malfunctioning lap bar, and her smile fades. "Is everything okay?"

"We can't find Paige," I tell her. "Have you heard from her tonight?"

Master Park shakes her head. "No. Why? Did something happen?"

Nikki goes through the scenario again, and I feel even worse at the second telling. I'm waiting for someone to come out of the shadows and hand me the Worst Dad of the Year award. When she finishes up, Master Park crosses the room and takes her cell phone from her purse.

"Who are you calling?" I ask, wholly expecting it to be CPS.

"Fer. He's out around town. Maybe he's bumped into her." She pauses when he answers. They have a brief exchange then she explains what happened. I'm looking for the nearest hole to crawl into when she perks up and smiles. "Oh! That's great!" She looks at us. "She's fine. She's with Fer at The Olive Branch."

"How on earth did— you know what? I don't care. Oh, thank goodness she's safe," I sigh so deep I feel like I'm deflating. Master Park ends the call, and everything is right with the world again. We thank her and head back to the car. Except, I can't bring myself to go home. I need to see for myself that she's fine.

I tell Kiku to drive to The Olive Branch. Five minutes later, I'm watching Paige through the restaurant window. She's smiling. She's laughing. She's... happy. Something in me shifts, and I begin to feel like less of a failure.

"This looks way better than prom," Nikki mentions, pushes the door open, and steps inside, waving Paige's purse at her. "Hey, dumbass! You forget something?"

*

Paige

"Shit!" I pat my body up and down, as if doing so will magically make this circus tent of a dress produce pockets with my purse inside. "I left my purse at prom." I look at Jet apologetically.

"Don't worry about it," he smiles, then jabs a thumb at Fer. "I'll just put it on his tab."

"What? Fuck that! She can have her own damned tab!" Fer complains as he finishes his second drink. We've only been here, like, fifteen minutes. I do some quick mental math and my eyes bug at his estimated weekly tab.

"Fine then, asshole, it'll just be on the house tonight."

I'm about to object when the restaurant door opens.

"Hey, dumbass! You forget something?"

I shift around on my barstool and see Nikki and Alpha approaching. Nikki's waving my purse at me, and Alpha... Alpha looks like he's had a rough night. I hop down and take my purse from Nikki. "What's going on? Why are you here?"

"Um, why are *you* here?" she asks, with mock upset. "You were supposed to catch the bus home and then text me. You never did, so I called Alpha; he freaked out, and we've been searching for you."

"Wow, way to be inconsiderate, Monkey," Fer snorts from his seat. I turn to glare at him and see Jet talking to Shiraz and another member of the staff. They vanish into the back of the restaurant.

I approach Alpha. He looks like a wreck. I guess I'd be too if I were him. "I'm sorry," I apologize and hug him. "I didn't mean to worry you."

"I thought I told you to call me if things didn't go well," he says to me and hugs me tighter.

"I know, but I was afraid you'd try and convince me to stay or something. I just... I just wanted to avoid the extra drama."

"Well, you sure fucked that up," Fer points out from the peanut gallery.

"Thank you, Captain Obvious," I groan.

"Happy to help."

"No, it's fine. I understand. I'm just glad you're safe," Alpha sighs, and looks at me. He's smiling, but it's a tired smile, and I feel terrible for him. "Things have been getting better, and I've just been so afraid I would screw up and we'd be back in the weeds again."

"Yeah," I agree. "Me too— that I'd screw up and ruin our progress— I mean. Not you."

"I'm sorry your prom didn't go well."

"I'm sorry I ruined your night." I look past him to Nikki. "And your night. You should be out having fun."

Nikki shakes her head and waves me off. "Nah. It's just a dance. I've been to a dance before. I'll survive missing one."

As we're talking, Shiraz and Jet are behind me stringing holiday lights across the walls, and a couple of the other patrons are stringing more up above some of the tables and booths.

"Clear out seven and eight," Jet says. The two center tables are pulled aside, opening up the restaurant floor. The house lights dim a bit, and the strings of lights twinkle. The song on the surround sound switches to some poppy dance music. Jet takes off his apron and approaches me.

"May I have this dance?" he asks, extending his hand.

"Are you fucking serious?" Fer asks, nearly choking on his drink.

"I didn't ask you," Jet retorts. "And yes, I'm serious. This one's missing her school dance to eat my food and hang out with you. It's the least I can do." He looks back at me. "What do you say?"

"I don't know how to dance," I reply.

"It's okay, neither do I. We'll figure it out."

I let Jet lead me to the makeshift dance floor and, once more, try to pull all my files on dancing. This time my cabinets open. Before I know it, I'm spinning, stepping, and looking like a huge dork, but I don't care. I feel good. I feel happy. Then I see Nikki drag Alpha onto the floor to dance with her. He is about as good a dancer as I'd expect, but hey, I'm no Misty Copeland, so I have no room to talk.

I look around the restaurant at the other customers and the staff. In all, there are maybe about a dozen or fifteen other people there. Their eyes are all glowing various shades of brown, green, and blue— it's beautiful— more beautiful than the fancy hologram ceiling at prom. At least, it is to me.

Out of the corner of my eye, the front door opens, and Master Park comes in. She looks around, a little confused, then approaches Fer. I don't know what they're talking about, but I see him smiling and she smiles back. Then they kiss, and it's sweet... in an ew-gross-she's-kissing-Fer kind of way, but they both look happy, and that makes me happy. After they say whatever it is they need to say, Master Park tries to convince Fer to dance with her. After some coaxing, they join us.

More tables move. The dance floor grows to accommodate the others who want to dance, too. Soon, it seems like the entire restaurant is dancing and every frightened, angry, sad thing inside me is quiet for once.

I may have lost my parents, but family, I'm learning, doesn't begin and end with my parents. Yeah, they're gone, and I'll probably never stop missing them, but looking out across Jet's small restaurant reminds me that my family is bigger and better than I ever dreamed it could be... and I don't think I'd have it any other way.

Girls' Night Out Part 3

Pursuit

ANJIKO LOOKED AROUND the open yard. "Any idea which way he went?" There was no fence closing the yard off from the neighbors, so the suspect could have taken off in any direction. She looked to her right toward the gravel driveway and saw it was still packed with vehicles. It was possible he could have driven off. She inspected the vehicles further, taking care to avoid the random piles of dog shit that were scattered all over the yard and found only one car with a Fort Thomas parking pass and ID hanging from the rearview mirror. He had to still be on foot.

She looked around the yard again; the ambient noise of the Friday evening traffic was disrupted by screeching tires and the angry blast of a car horn further down the block.

Both scrappers took off in the direction of the sound. As they ran, Ino pulled her phone from her pocket again and sent the drone to scout ahead. Anjiko glanced over and saw Ino glued to her phone, studying the footage. She turned her attention back to the sidewalk in front of her and barely dodged a lamp post. She glanced over to Ino again and saw her, still absorbed in the drone footage, avoid the same lamp post without looking up. Then she stepped off the curb into the street.

"Pedestrians, Anjiko," she said, her voice sounding bored and distracted.

Anjiko looked over and saw a man pushing a baby stroller down the sidewalk with one hand and holding his toddler's hand in the other.

"Oh, jeeze, my bad!" she apologized, stopping just before she collided with the stroller. She looked up at the man who had pulled the toddler off the sidewalk and into his arms and smiled. The man did not smile back. "Sorry, I don't know how she does that."

The man was not amused and just glared harder as the baby, upon noticing they were no longer moving, started to cry, while the toddler squealed in her tiny, giddy voice, "A robot! She's a robot!"

"I'm not a robot, kid," Anjiko said, dodging the barrage of tiny fingers that were trying to poke her. Suddenly, a message flashed on her HUD from Ino.

"The drone found him. What's your hold up?"

She blinked away the message and turned back to the man. The baby was quiet now, sucking on a pacifier, but the toddler was squirming like a cat about to get a bath, in her father's arms. She reached toward Anjiko with growing agitation demanding to touch the 'robot girl's' glowing eyes. Anjiko sighed and leaned in close toward the girl, but just out of her reach.

"Uh-oh! Danger, Will Robinson," she said, sounding like she was talking to an excited puppy instead of a small human on the verge of a tantrum. "That term is not cool. Oh no, no, no. We don't use that word when we talk about people like me. Do we? No, we don't." She looked at the father, her tone and expression stern. "Do better, man." Then she took off down the road to catch up to Ino.

Anjiko caught up to Ino about a block away in front of a clothing boutique. They were nearing the courthouse square, and the civilian traffic was becoming thicker and thicker the closer they got.

"Well, where's our guy?" Anjiko asked and looked at the footage from over Ino's shoulder.

"What were you doing back there?" Ino asked, not answering the question.

"Civilian education," Anjiko grinned, and asked again, "So, where's he at?"

"Not far. Heading west on Kirkwood."

Anjiko leaned over the petite blonde's shoulder and looked at the digital map on the phone.

"That's him," Ino pointed to one of the civilians who was moving faster than the others in a straight line down the street.

Anjiko leaned in closer, and Ino batted her away. "Hey, can that drone identify other scrappers?" she asked.

"Yes, why?"

"Can it scan that building there?"

"Yes, but—" Ino stopped herself and held the phone up for Anjiko to see. "Oh, it looks like Fer's there."

"I knew it!" she cheered. "Come on, let's get after this guy!"

As they ran, Anjiko sent a message to Fer's HUD.

"Hey, I'm gonna need you to step outside onto the sidewalk in exactly five seconds."

Less than a second later Fer replied, *"Why?"*

"Because of reasons. Four... three..."

"Fine. I'm going."

The two rounded the corner just in time to see Fer step out onto the sidewalk and Vincent plow right into him. The skinny human bounced off Fer's brick wall of a torso and fell backward onto the pavement, bouncing his head on the concrete.

"What the hell?" Fer exclaimed when he saw Anjiko and Ino coming at him in a dead sprint.

"Oh, good job, Fer-Fer! You caught him!" Anjiko cheered.

"I did what now?" Fer looked at Ino for some context.

"We've been pursuing this criminal for about four blocks now. Thank you for your assistance, Captain."

"Criminal?" He looked at the moaning human on the sidewalk. He hadn't been told about any such assignment. "Are you sure? You're not taking up LARPing again, are you, Ino? You remember how that turned out last time."

Ino sighed and recalled her overzealous participation in a local role-playing group four years prior. "I am still paying for the damages, yes. But, no, this is not that. This man is a criminal, and if you don't mind, we would appreciate your help getting him back to Fort Thomas so we can question him."

The door to the restaurant beside them opened, and a synthetic woman in a black concert t-shirt and apron poked her head out.

"Fer, your order's up." Then she saw the human lying on the sidewalk and became concerned. "Hey, is everything okay out here?"

"It's fine, Shiraz. Box my stuff up to go and put it on my tab. I'll pay it tomorrow."

The server nodded and was just about to go back inside when Anjiko stopped her.

"Ooh, can I get margarita to go, please?" she asked, much to Ino's annoyance. Anjiko noted her friend's exasperation and amended her statement. "Make it two," she smiled, pleased with herself. "And put it on his tab."

GHOSTS OF CHRISTMAS PAST

"Heads up, Iron Man! He's headed your way!" Sergeant Hemingway's voice booms in my earpiece, and I look through my scope. I'm positioned on top of an abandoned drugstore in some ghetto in Saint Louis which I know doesn't narrow it down much, on Christmas Eve. It's my first Christmas, actually ...well first since I woke up. It's been snowing for the last three days and everything below me is a dirty sludge the color of soaked newspaper. I'm still new to having my own opinions and right now, my strongest is that snow in a city is possibly one of the most depressing things I've ever seen. The other is that even the clean stuff is obnoxious when you've been laying in it for almost thirty minutes which I've been doing. Everything from my waist down is cold and damp.

According to the intel from Captain Fabron, some assembly line synthetic corrupted about a week ago, trashed everyone and everything on its line, and bolted. A couple days ago, area civilians were saying something big and mean was attacking people at random in a nearby neighborhood. So, here we are; me and my eight human squadmates.

I've only been a member of Rho squad for about a month, and we're out in the CZ putting down corruptions. It's shitty work, but I'm good at it; we all are, and this place needs people like us in a bad way.

There's a crash, a musical shattering of glass whose source I can't see, and almost instantly, half a dozen civilians flee into my line of sight. I ignore them. They're not my priority.

From around the corner, a car soars through the air and hits the pavement with a strangely satisfying crunch. The thing playing shot-put with the Buick, yeah, that's my priority. I hear more footsteps pounding against the wet pavement below me and peer over my rocket launcher. I can see Sergeant Hemingway sprinting from one form of cover to the next. I watch him move from behind a pile of plowed snow and ice to a parked car where he stops and raises his side arm.

"I'm gonna lead him right to you, got it?" I hear him in my ear. "He's a big motherfucker, so don't hold back."

He's not kidding. About 10 meters down the road, I can see a massive brute of a machine lumber into view. His skyn's torn in more places than not, and I can see its arms are nothing more than two giant, steel pistons. No wonder it can throw a fucking car. I peer through my scope, and I can see its face. There's a constant white steam coming from its nose. It's probably overheating or at least running on more power than it's used to, and its eyes are wild with the same insane rage I've seen a dozen times before on corruptions.

I don't know what happened to make this thing a walking murder factory instead of just another free-thinking machine like me and the others back at Fort Thomas. No one knows why Jane fails at waking some of us up; and I don't care. What I do care about is that Sergeant Hemingway is standing on top of that car now, shooting at it like some dumbass cowboy. I like Sergeant Hemingway, but he tends to act like he's invincible. I think he believes he is.

"You better start running or that thing's gonna smear you all over the street," I say into my mic because I know for a fact humans are not invincible. They're not even very durable, to be honest. Fuck, most of them are downright fragile.

"Nah, it's fine," he replies. His voice is relaxed like he's done this a hundred times.

I watch the corrupt synthetic pick up and launch another car. This one soars over Sergeant Hemingway's head and crashes through a diner window. The screams are deafening, and I hope no one is hurt.

"Okay, maybe not so fine," Sarge says, somewhat anxious now, and hops down from the car. "Hey, Gomez, I could use a lift outta here if you'd be so kind."

"You know, I'm starting to get tired of bailing your ass out, Sergeant." I hear Specialist Gomez's voice on my earpiece. It's deep and has all the smoothness of a bucket of gravel. I like Gomez. She takes absolutely no shit and can drive like a pro.

"You know you love it," Sarge says back when the Humvee comes into sight. "Watch out for Mongo there; he likes to throw his toys."

I see the Humvee plowing down the street leaving a wake of sludgy tread marks. Gomez speeds past the corrupt with no trouble, taking a few extra seconds to maneuver the truck into throwing a wave of slush at it. Like I said, she's a badass behind the wheel. As such, she seems to be more successful at leading the big guy toward me than Sarge.

"Hey, you guys better get the hell out of here. That thing's coming straight for you," I inform them.

"Roger that," Gomez says. Then she leans out the window and blows me a kiss. It's nothing special; she does this to everyone. From what I've gathered, it's kind of her thing. I like it; it suits her. "Blow 'em sky high, Iron Man."

And I do. As soon as Gomez and Sarge are out of the way I zero my sites in on Mongo and fire. The rocket hits but doesn't do the damage we had all hoped. Instead of a smoldering hole in its chest, I've got a supremely pissed off machine with one missing arm ...and a partridge in a pear tree. But it's fine. This is fine. It just means I get to show off a little now. And I gotta admit, I love showing off.

I put my rocket launcher down and get to my feet. Below me Mongo— Jesus, where does Sergeant Hemingway come up with these fucking awful names? Probably the same place he came up with Iron Man. But, whatever. Anyway, Mongo's down on the ground, one arm socket sparking like an illegal firework, trying to rip a streetlight out of the sidewalk. I do a couple quick calculations on distance, get a running start, and leap off the top of the building.

I hit the ground with a force that would shatter my squadmates' legs and take off straight for Mongo. The brute sees me coming and abandons its attempt to uproot the streetlight in favor of crushing me like a pop can. The corrupt raises its massive steel arm above its head and moves to bring it down on me. But Mongo's big— way bigger than me— and that makes it slow. Now, I'm no sprinter, but my ankles and knees have some pretty nice hydraulics, if I do say so, and I'm in the clear before it even finishes its swing.

I wind up off to the side while Mongo tries to recover from the swing.

It's hunched and off balance with its head almost at my height. I figure if I can get it on the ground, I can put a bullet or six in its power supply. Not wasting any time, I cock my arm back and attack. My fist collides with its head, and I can feel its teeth break. The corrupt staggers sideways and hunches even lower, so I swing again with my left. This time, I connect a little higher, and now its right optic is flickering like a green strobe light. I hike my knee up and push my boot forward into its chest with a grunt. Mongo falls onto its back, and I lean over the crazed machine with my pistol drawn. I train my weapon on its broad, heaving chest. As my finger wraps around the trigger, I hear a series of quick hissing noises, like short bursts of air escaping a pressurized chamber. I pull my trigger just as the piston on its arm releases right under me.

*

I'm not in the snow anymore. It's dark and I'm lying on a bed or cot of some kind. My chest feels…wrong… and my boot cycle is sluggish. Despite not being fully operational yet, I hear voices. They're garbled at first, like they're talking under water, but after a few seconds, they become clearer.

"Jesus, Hem, whattaya doin' goin' and breakin' the new guy?" The voice belongs to Specialist Grabowski, our squad medic.

"Shit, I didn't break anything. Don't you go pinning this on me."

I try to speak to let Grabowski know it wasn't Sarge's fault, but I can't move. I guess my audio sensors are the only things online. It shouldn't take this long to power up.

"Look, it's your plan, your responsibility. That's what Cap'n Fabron's always sayin'."

"Don't quote Captain Fabron to me, Grabowski, just fix him."

"Fix him? I'm a medic, Hem, I fix people. The human kind. This guy, I dunno, this guy needs a goddamned auto mechanic or IT guy or somethin'. Probably both."

My optics begin to come back online, and everything is all pixelated; it's like the entire world's been turned into an old school video game. For a moment, I'm worried I might have been damaged worse than I thought, and my optics can only manage sixteen-bit resolution. Then I feel Grabowski thump the side of my head and everything is back in full focus.

"Hey, hey! Caveman technology! Works every time," he cheers. I look at him and blink a few times while the rest of my systems finally lurch back online.

I look around. I'm not in the street anymore. I'm back at Fort Shelley in the medical center. I'm lying on a stretcher, and I can feel the tiny cable attached to the back of my neck. I follow it to Grabowski's power-house medical computer sitting on a table nearby. Man, he mustn't know what to do with me if he's got me hardwired. The only reason I'd need to be physically connected to anything is if I were really busted. That last thought sinks in fast, and I'm worried. Am I really busted? I look at the monitor and see me. Well, lines of my data anyway, indicating which of my systems are operational and which ones are damaged.

"How did I get here?" I ask, raising myself into a sitting position. Grabowski's look of accomplishment vanishes. He turns to his screen with Sarge over his shoulder.

"Whaddaya can't remember?" Grabowski asks me nervously. "Uh, w-what's your name?"

I don't officially have a name, so I reply with the most obvious thing to me. "SRN: six-two-seven-eight."

Sarge growls and rolls his eyes. "Not your number. Your name. What. Is. Your. Name?"

I don't know. Again, I don't have an actual name. They all just call me… aaw, shit. Seriously? "Is it Iron Man? I don't want it to be Iron Man. I hate Iron Man," I mumble. And I do. I really hate being called Iron Man. I like it better when Captain Fabron calls me Homme de Fer, or usually just Fer for short. And I get that Homme de Fer and Iron Man are literally the same thing, but Fabron's speech is this wild Frankenstein's monster of English and French and it just sounds so much cooler.

"Alright, fine, whatever. Where are you?"

"Confederated Zone base, Fort Shelley. Columbia, Missouri."

"Who am I?"

"Sergeant Victor Hemingway."

He runs his fingers dramatically through the curly orange mop on the top of his head. "Damn right I am." He points to Grabowski. "Who's that nerd?"

"Specialist Justin Grabowski. Squad medic."

"And IT guy, it seems," Grabowski adds as he types at his computer.

"See, he's fine," Sarge says to Grabowski and pats my shoulder like it's the fender of a car. Then I see his eyes trail to my torso and his smile falters. I look down. My heavy jacket has been removed. I'm in my t-shirt, and I see a dent the size of a dinner plate in the center of my chest. "Well, fine enough."

"I… I can't work like this," I say as I gape at the veritable crater in my frame. No wonder I took so long to boot up. I'm amazed I'm able to operate at all.

"What? Nah, it's fine. We'll get one of the guys from motor pool down here with one of those heavy-duty suction cup things, and you know," he makes a popping sound with his mouth, "Pop that dent right out. No problem." He turns to Grabowski. "No problem." Grabowski does not share his confidence.

"How in the heck did you ever make Sergeant? Honestly, how?"

Sarge shrugs. "Good looks and sass, I guess."

Despite my current situation, I laugh at this. He may be dumb as a brick when it comes to how I work, but Sergeant Hemingway is funny. That's why everyone likes him. It's why I like him.

"Okay, so, on the surface everything seems fine," Grabowski says to me, then double takes at my chest. "I mean, like, internally. Your memory drives all seem fine. You took a while to power up, though. Might just be a one-time thing from being cold cocked all the way back to the FORTRAN days. The diagnostics still need to finish running, so we'll know more later."

"How long will that take?" I ask.

Grabowski looks at his computer. "Two, maybe three hours? I mean, you're pretty complicated; there's a lot to check."

I watch Grabowski get to his feet and head for the exit. "Just sit tight. I'll be back to check on ya. I'm gonna go to the rec room."

Sarge follows him across the med center. "Hey, tell Picos to get her stash of booze and bring it down. We may be at Shitty Shelley, but Christmas is Christmas."

I hear Grabowski give a reply to the affirmative before he disappears out the door. Sarge is about to leave, as well, when Captain Fabron walks in. Fabron is a big guy. All muscle. All accent. Alright in my book.

"Where are you going, Sergeant?" I hear him ask.

"To the rec room, Captain. Me and the team are planning on having a little Christmas party."

"Yeah, don't mind me," I hear Grabowski holler back. "I'll just sit in the corner and play with my dreidel."

"Don't be shitty, Grabowski. It's not my fault we got the cooler holiday," Sarge says.

"Your holiday revolves around an obese, geriatric demi-god who stalks kids," Grabowski counters.

Sarge laughs, then turns back to Captain Fabron. "You gonna join us, Cap?"

Captain Fabron crosses his arms over his chest. He looks at Sarge then at me. I pretend to not pay attention. I don't mean to eavesdrop, but I can hear a pin drop in a padded room. I don't think they realize that.

"What about him?" Captain Fabron asks.

"What about him? Diagnostics are running. Should be done in about three hours. Everything else is just cosmetic."

"So, he will not be joining you and the rest of the team for your little party?" He says the word 'little', and it sounds like 'leedle'.

"Well, no. He's hooked up to—"

"Why don't you sit with him until the diagnostics are finished?"

"Aw, come on, Cap!"

"Sergeant, I feel I need to remind you the only reason he is in medical at all is because of your plan to use yourselves as bait and him as the strong man."

"But it worked."

"It didn't work if it ended with an injured teammate. You need to understand, he is not a tool or a weapon. He's a person. He's just as much a Rho as you or me, and you need to treat him as such."

"Cap—"

"So, you're going to stay here with your teammate, so he doesn't have to spend Christmas Eve alone. Am I understood?"

"Yes, Sir."

Captain Fabron leaves and Sarge turns and stares at me. His expression is one of someone who knows they deserve to sleep in the bed they've made but isn't happy about it. He crosses the room and takes a seat on Grabowski's chair and looks at the data on the screen. I don't know what to say to him.

"So," Sarge finally speaks. His green eyes bore into me, and it's hard to look at him. "You really don't like being called Iron Man?"

The question catches me off guard, and I laugh. Of all the things I was expecting him to say, that was not it. "No," I reply. "I don't."

Sarge looks indignant and rolls the chair closer to me. "What? Why? Iron Man's a great name."

"It is if you're a narcissistic billionaire on a team of costumed weirdos."

"Woah! Are you tellin' me you don't like The Avengers?" He raises an eyebrow.

This question sounds serious, and judging by Sarge's expression, his future opinion of me hinges on how I answer. I'm feeling nervous about being put on the spot like this. I've only heard of The Avengers in passing; my knowledge of them is garnered mostly from internet memes and TV commercials. I don't like or dislike The Avengers; I nothing them.

"I don't think I have enough information on them to make a decision," I reply slowly and await his response. Sarge considers my words for a long, silent moment. He bobs his head up and down, and his curls bounce a little as he does.

"Alright, alright, that's fair," he says. "We'll work on that when we get home. You'll see. You're gonna love being called Iron Man."

"Yeah, I doubt that. It's a stupid name, and I don't like it," I say again.

Sarge rolls his eyes and pulls a pack of cigarettes and a dull black Zippo from his pocket. "Fine, then, if Iron Man's so god awful, what should we call you?"

"Fer," I say after a few seconds. "I like it when Captain Fabron calls me Fer."

"You realize that's fucking stupid, right? It's literally the same damn thing," he says and lights a cigarette. I know for a fact smoking is not allowed in the med center, but I decide not to say anything.

"It sounds better in French. That, and I won't get confused for an Avenger."

"I'd want to be confused for an Avenger," Sarge muses and suddenly he's offering me his pack of cigarettes. "Here, have a smoke with me."

I stutter a reply that sounds like my speech is glitching. Is he serious? He can't be serious. I'm a machine and machines aren't designed to smoke. Granted, we're also not designed to have opinions and emotions, but here we are.

Sarge pushes the small white and blue box forward. "C'mon. Cap says

I need to start treating you like the rest of the squad, so, here." He nudges the box at me again, and I pull one of the cigarettes out. I place it between my lips, and he lights it for me. I watch Sarge take a long drag on his, and I follow suit, but instead of exhaling a smooth cloud of smoke like him, I'm coughing so hard I almost pull Grabowski's whole computer setup off the table. The smoke burns my respiration tubes, and I can already tell my body is not okay with it because there's a constant, thin stream of smoke coming from my nostrils as my ventilation system flushes it all out.

"That's fucking awful!" I exclaim, still coughing a little. The burning subsides, and my ventilation kicks off; I am no longer a smoke tower. "How do you do this all day, Sergeant?"

"Eh, you get used to it. And call me Hem. Everyone else does." Sarge grins and rolls back over to Grabowski's computer. "I wonder if I can stream movies on this thing." He takes another drag off his cigarette. I, however, opt to pinch mine out between my thumb and forefinger and flick it into a nearby trash bin.

"I don't see why you couldn't," I reply.

"Well, I don't want to screw up whatever Grabowski's doing with you on here."

I get up from the stretcher and crouch down beside Sarge…er… Hem. I take the keyboard from him and start navigating around all of Grabowski's diagnostics programs.

"Must be pretty weird, working on a computer that has your brain on the screen."

"Yeah, it's pretty meta," I nod and bring up Netflix on the monitor. "There. And I didn't even trigger my self-destruct mechanism." Hem looks at me, and I can tell he's not sure if I'm being serious or not. "Really?" I scoff. "C'mon, I don't have a self-destruct mechanism. How *did* you make sergeant?" I ask, reiterating Grabowski's earlier question.

"I already told you guys, good looks and sass."

I look him over. Good looks might be a bit of a stretch. His frame is short and lean; petite, I guess, would be the best word. His hair is a bright orange high and tight topped with a mess of curls. He's got thick orange eyebrows and a face full of freckles making him look perpetually adolescent even though he's in his early 20's.

"If you say so," I reply.

"I do say so," he says and takes the keyboard back from me. His fingers start pecking at the keys, and I can hear him whispering, "Come on, come on, have it," as he types. He hits enter and holds his breath. A second later, he lets out a whoop of excitement. On the monitor is the image of a gruff-looking man in a white tank top holding a pistol at the ready with a twilight cityscape behind him. "Mother fuckin' *Die Hard*."

"*Die Hard*?" I ask.

"Yep. It's only the greatest Christmas movie of all time."

I consider the image again and feel compelled to point out the obvious. "It doesn't look like a Christmas movie."

Hem whips around and faces me again. "You shut your whore mouth!" he says, jamming his finger into my chest—which proves to be more awkward than we expect, as his finger keeps going until it reaches the bottom of the dent there.

We both laugh at his stupid, failed gesture, and he clicks the play icon. We're barely through the opening credits when we hear Specialist Sunshine Picos call to us from the doorway.

"Hey, Hem, whatcha doing in here?" She asks, holding a sleeve of red plastic cups in one hand and a heavy looking bottle of apple juice in the other— except, it's definitely not apple juice. "Grabowski said you said to bust out the care pack my sister sent." She strolls into the med center and approaches us. "Oh shit! Is that *Die Hard*?!" She perches herself on the stretcher beside me and elbows me playfully. "Glad you're okay, Iron Man."

"Ah, ah, we're not calling him that anymore," Hem says, still fixated on the movie. "He doesn't like it."

Picos looks at me like a sad little kitten. "Aaw. But what're we gonna call you?"

I look at Hem, and he looks back at me with an approving nod. "My name's Fer," I say and feel stupid and bold at the same time.

"Well, shit, why didn't you say something earlier? Here we are calling you something you hate like a bunch of assholes." She hops off the stretcher and puts the jug down. Then, she pulls three cups from the sleeve and pours a little of the deep brown liquid into each. She hands one to Hem, keeps one for herself, and hands the third to me. "Drink up, Fer," she grins. Much like with the cigarette, I'm not prepared for my systems to rebel at the alcohol. I sputter a few times and thank her. "That's my big guy," she says patting my back like a choking toddler. "Good stuff, huh?"

"Better than the cigarette," I choke, and she bursts into riotous laughter.

"Oh, Hem, are you trying to make him your own personal mini-me?"

"Look at him, Picos," Hem snorts, still glued to the movie. "What about him is mini?"

We all share a good laugh; I am kind of big compared to most of them. A few minutes later, Miller and Oxford come by looking for Picos since she hadn't come back to the rec room with her booze. They both wind up grabbing chairs and joining us around the computer. Miller's wearing a Santa hat until Hem mentions something about her not being the rookie anymore. She fist-pumps and gets up from her seat to place the hat on my head. "Merry Christmas, Rookie Claus," she says and pinches my cheek.

"Um, thanks?" I laugh and Picos pours her and Oxford each a drink.

One by one the entire squad migrates into medical with me and Hem. Picos pours drinks and they pull up chairs crowding around Grabowski's computer.

"Hey, where is the party?" Captain Fabron asks, ambushing us all. "I thought you were all in the rec room. I had pizza delivered, but no one was there."

"We were, Sir," Picos replies. "But Hem and Fer are watching *Die Hard*, so we sort of changed the venue."

"Fer?" Captain Fabron asks and looks at me. "So, I see you've given yourself a name for Christmas. That is good. It makes you officially one of the family. Welcome to Rho, Fer. We're happy to have you."

I see everyone look up at me and raise their cups. They don't say anything, but their faces get their point across. I'm one of the family. I smile and raise my cup back to them, and we all take a drink together.

"And every time a bell rings, and angel gets his wings," Hem says in a high pitched, childish tone. "Now, c'mon shut up, you're all ruining the movie with your big, gross feelings."

A few of us give Hem some shit, and we all go back to watching the movie. Captain Fabron moves the pizza from the rec room to medical, and we all have the most ridiculous, amazing, perfectly Rho Christmas dinner I can remember.

*

And I still remember it. I hold the old Santa hat in my hands as I sit on the sofa in my apartment. Picos' booze was terrible, and the pizza was cold by the time Fabron moved it down to us, but we honestly didn't care. We were in the middle of the raging fucktangle that is the CZ, stuck at Shitty Shelley for Christmas, having the best damned holiday I think any of us ever had.

On the coffee table in front of me, I have our squad picture and nine shots poured out for them. The ninth is for Onda. She came in about a year later and not only replaced me as the rookie, but she was also another synthetic.

I rifle through my old footlocker. After... well, after— we'll just leave it at that— I was given a few of their possessions. I got last pick after all the families. I pick up Gomez's sunglasses. The lenses are cracked and one of the temples is missing, but I polish them gently and put them down by her shot glass. Next, I take out a beat-up medic patch and sit it by Grabowski's shot glass. The next item I retrieve is Picos' flask. It's silver with our squad insignia etched into it on one side and 'Picos' on the other. One by one, I take out the only physical reminders of my old squad that I have and place them beside their assigned shot glasses. I have Jones's boonie cap, Oxford's crushed to hell and back cell phone, Miller's pet rock, Judgey. Judgey was sort of our unofficial mascot. The slide from Onda's side arm, and Captain Fabron's pocketknife. Then I reach in for the final item. I pull out a matte-black Zippo lighter. On one side the words, 'Hem: Fort Shitty Shelley' are scratched into it. I stare at it for a long time then use it to light the cigarette hanging between my lips. I sit the lighter down and stare at my pitiful treasures.

I miss them. They were my family in a way the Omegas can never be. I got my name with them. I learned how to navigate personhood with them. We were heroes together. We took some lives and saved a lot more. Then, one day, they were gone. Ripped away from this world in a maelstrom of rubble and fire. And while their souls— if there is such a thing— are at rest, their memories are still very much alive, and I miss them.

I take a drag from my cigarette and exhale a smooth cloud of smoke; I'm much better at handling cigarettes these days. "So," I say to the line of oddities on my coffee table. "It's Christmas Eve. How's *Die Hard* sound?"

Girls' Night Out Part 4

Conclusion

VINCENT MAY SAT, uneasy, on the hard metal folding chair inside the Omega's interrogation room. He rubbed the goose egg on the back of his head and winced. Across the table, he saw all three Omegas looking at him.

Vincent knew the Omegas, well, knew of them. Who didn't? They were the ones you called when you wanted something taken care of quick and dirty, or so everyone said. Their missions were always classified, and they were some of the only synthetic scrappers on base who had been to the West and made it back to tell about it. They were also the ones who had taken out that nut-job, Joshua, awhile back, and everyone knew what kind of beast he was. He'd heard, and this was just a rumor, mind you, they had to blow him up with a truck full of C-4 before he finally went down for keeps. A *truck* of C-4.

They were legends.

They were lunatics.

And they were sitting right in front of him.

Vincent May was screwed.

He knew what he had done, and he had been a fool to think he would get away with it. Maybe if it had been the pink-haired one, she was the least threatening, well, more or less. Could someone who supposedly carried explosives in her pocket actually be qualified as unthreatening?

Nope, it had to be the Reader whom he crossed. Goddamn, she was freaky. And the stuff she could do just by looking? Yikes. He shuddered and crossed his legs tight. He wanted to have kids one day, and there was no way to do that if she irradiated his bits and pieces with her X-ray vision because that's what he'd heard she did when she looked at you. Her eyes lit up all crazy and green— radioactive green— and she could see everything inside you, even your thoughts. He'd heard the reason there were so few synthetics like her was because of the radiation she gave off.

"So, are we gonna get this show on the road or what?" their captain asked. Vincent cowered at the sound of his voice. Oh, he'd heard of their captain too. Well, their new captain. The old one— the tall, handsome one who actually seemed normal— was off in the CZ. This new guy looked like he was programmed with only one mood, and it was bad. He had scars on his face and looked like he needed a shave. He'd never tell him that, of course, because he also looked like he could rip someone's spine out through their nose and use it like a jump rope.

"I mean, this guy looks like he's about to wet himself," Fer continued. "C'mon Ino, what the hell did he do?"

Ino was just about to speak when she was cut off by a long, loud slurping noise. She narrowed her eyes and looked at Anjiko who was sucking up the last drops of the canned cocktail in her hand.

"This is not the same as a real margarita," she grouched at Fer. "You lied. Ino, why didn't you tell me he was lying?"

"You know open container laws are a real thing in this state, right? You can't just get an actual margarita to go," Fer explained.

Anjiko looked at the empty can. She crushed it and sat it down with a hollow *tink* on the edge of the table. "This can-a-rita tastes like someone made lime Kool-Aid with battery acid."

"If you didn't like it, you could have just thrown it out," Fer said.

"Well, that would just be wasteful, wouldn't it?"

"Excuse me, people? Can we please focus?" Ino snapped and turned to the cowering human in front of them.

"Look," Vincent began. "I'm really sorry for what I did. I shouldn't have done it, and I regret it now."

"No, you don't. You regret getting caught. If you regretted what you did, you would have confessed as soon as you did it." Ino leaned across the table, and Vincent leaned back in his chair to keep away from her. "There's a difference."

Vincent closed his eyes, crossed his legs, and held onto the edge of the folding chair. He looked like he was either awaiting a firing squad or fighting to keep his sphincter clenched against some kind of disastrous bowel movement. "Oh god, please don't zap me! I'm sorry! I'll never do it again! Please! I have a dog; he needs me to give him his seizure medication—"

"That was your dog?" Anjiko interrupted, recalling the obnoxious Pomeranian from earlier and the yard full of its messes. "You need to clean up after it better because your yard is disgusting."

"I— I will, I promise. Just please don't fry me—"

"Wait." This time it was Fer who interrupted. "Just what does he think you're going to do to him, Ino?" He turned to Vincent with an amused grin. "Seriously, I gotta know. What does your squishy little brain think she's gonna do?"

Vincent frowned and swallowed hard. "She's gonna use her X-ray eyes and zap me. I'll probably get radiation poisoning or be sterilized or something."

Fer let out a single, loud, "Ha!" Then, slapped Ino on the back. "I swear, the rumors about you are getting better all the time. What next? Is she gonna suck out your soul or just fry your mind like Pennywise's Deadlights? Do you read Stephen King, Vincent?"

"N—no. No, Sir."

Fer shook his head. "Shame."

"I— You mean she doesn't..."

"I didn't say that," he smirked, not wanting to spoil the gloriously extravagant rumor mill. "Now, come on, just tell me what you did so I can get on with my life."

Vincent screwed up his lips into a tight, knotty frown and looked at the floor. "I tooermaretti," he mumbled so low and fast it was impossible to discern what was said.

"I'm sorry, you what?" Fer asked.

Vincent took a deep breath and braced himself. "I took her amaretti. Okay?"

"Her what?"

"Amaretti! He ate my amaretti!" Ino repeated.

"An ama-whatti?"

"He ate all my amaretti!"

"What? No! I only took one. I was hungry, and there were like a dozen in the bag. I figured you wouldn't miss one. I guess you did. I'm sorry."

"It may have started with one, but you came back and ate them all! I get a bag of them sent to me every year from an old colleague in Lazio, and you ate them all!"

"I swear I didn't! I was only in your common room on Wednesday. You can ask anyone. You can check the security cameras! I swear!"

Ino's eyes lit up and Vincent almost dove under the table.

"I don't know how you're doing it," Ino stood up and leaned over the table, eyes still glowing. "But you're tricking me. I know you're lying!"

"I'm not!"

"You are!"

"Alright, alright, Ino, calm down before the poor guy has a stroke or something," Fer said. Ino's eyes dimmed, and she sat down with a huff, allowing Fer to continue. "Now, first, what the hell is an amaretti, and why is it important enough to use Section tech and time on?"

"Ooh, ooh, I know!" Anjiko's hand shot up. "They're little almond cookies."

"What?" Fer squeezed his eyes shut, and bit his lower lip. "You mean to tell me you hunted this guy down, chased him through town, and used equipment worth more than all of us combined so you could scare him into admitting he ate your cookies?!"

"You say that like I chased him down over some of your processed American Oreos or something!" Ino argued. "These are different."

"Yeah," Anjiko agreed. "They're about this big and wrapped in these cute little colorful wrappers." She held up her hand and made a circle with her fingers about two inches wide. "They're soooo good."

Fer blinked a few times looking as though a switch had been flipped in his head. "Oh, those? Yeah, no, those are fucking delicious. I had like four of them yesterday, and probably five more the day before."

Ino cocked her head to one side and stared at Fer, fuming. "What?"

Fer looked back at her and smiled innocently, realizing his blunder all too late. "What? I didn't say anything."

As Fer unsuccessfully backpedaled, trying to hold off Ino, Anjiko rounded the table to Vincent. "I think you can go now," she said. "But, uh, we'd really appreciate it if you just kept this whole mess between us.

We'll send you some cash for the hole in your wall, too. Just, you know…"
She motioned like she was zipping her lips shut. "Cool?"

Vincent gave her a kind of dazed nod like he was just waking from a dream. "Yeah, sure. Whatever."

"Good," Anjiko replied. "Anyway, wanna grab a margarita?"

Terms and Conditions

"You've got to exercise a little restraint. Why is that so hard for you?" Alpha paced the floor in the Omega's briefing room. He looked at the slick black tabletop in the center of the room where just twenty minutes prior, the holographic image of Hedy Walker, Bloomington's new Chief of Police, stood voicing a laundry list of complaints about a certain Omega Captain.

On the other side of the table sat Fer, boots up on the arm of what used to be Nix's chair, looking bored.

"It's not hard. I exercise restraint all the time," he said.

Alpha stopped pacing and stared at him. Outside, the trees rustled in the wind that had been ramping up all afternoon. "You called her officers…" he trailed off, recalling Chief Walker's accusation. He didn't want to repeat the words. Swearing always made him feel awkward— this was largely because he never got it right— but he had a point to prove, so he cleared his throat and continued. "You called her officers a gaggle of cock-for-brains fuckwits not even fit for latrine duty."

Fer straightened up and nodded. "Yeah," he agreed. "But what I wanted to say was they were a gaggle of cock-for-brains fuckwits not even fit to shovel their own shit for sandwiches. See? Restraint."

Alpha opened his mouth to speak but found no words came out. Fer had, at long last, rendered him speechless. He squeezed his eyes shut and pinched the bridge of his nose like he had a headache. "Why?" he finally managed. "Why are you like this?"

"Like what? Look, Chief Blackburn never had an issue with me. We worked together fine for the last three years. It's not my fault his successor likes to clutch her pearls at a little salty language."

"A little salty? No. The fries in the civilian mess are a little salty." Alpha put his hands down on the tabletop and leaned toward him. "Your language is an unprofessional garbage heap of insults, inappropriate expletives, and derogatory slurs. The fact that it's actually taken this long for someone to file a formal complaint against you, quite frankly, astounds me."

"Me too," Fer agreed. "I mustn't have been trying hard enough." He chuckled and uncrossed and recrossed his legs on Nix's chair.

"Captain!" Alpha snapped, smacking the tabletop. "I don't think you're grasping the seriousness of this situation."

Fer straightened up and took his feet from the chair leaving behind a set of dusty tread marks on the arm. The boss was mad now and if there was one thing he hated, it was being around Alpha when he was in a bad mood. Bad Mood Alpha would often try to express his frustration by swearing, and Fer wasn't sure if he had it in him not to laugh at a sincerely angry but ultimately ineffective delivery of 'God shit it!' or 'What the damn is wrong with you?' "Okay, fine. Fine," Fer conceded. "I'll watch my language."

Alpha sighed and sat down in the chair across from him; his anger seeming to have subsided. "I'd like to believe you, but, unfortunately, I can't. You need to take serious steps to change your behavior."

"Oh yeah? Like how?" Fer caught Alpha's glare at the indignance in his voice, and he corrected himself with an exasperated sigh, "Like how, Sir?"

"There is software you can download that will help you censor your language and enhance your professionalism."

"Is that what you use?" Fer scoffed. Alpha raised a threatening eyebrow. "No? Oh, wait! I know! It's Nix, isn't it? I bet he uses shit like that and that's why he was everybody's favorite Captain."

Alpha considered the words and nodded. "As a matter of fact, he did for a while when he first took on the role. You and I both know he can have a temper, and the software helped him maintain his professionalism when things pushed his buttons. Once he found his stride, he uninstalled it."

Fer found himself wondering if he had been one of those button-pushers; he hoped he was. Oh, who was he kidding, he knew he was, and that made him feel all warm and fuzzy inside.

Alpha tapped the tabletop, and it lit up. Between the two of them was the image of a file folder. Alpha reached up and tapped it. The folder opened and four smaller images appeared below it. They all looked like logos for various software developers. He reached out to the one for American Robotics and made a slight throwing motion with his hand like he was waving it in Fer's direction. A second later, the icon popped up on Fer's HUD. "That's the info for the software he used. There are many programs like it; you can check them all out and choose one that suits you. But this is the one I recommend."

Fer stood up, pursing his lips, and shaking his head. "Do I have to?"

Alpha straightened up, and even though he was shorter and smaller in build than Fer, his authority was always broadcast loud and clear. "Yes. That's an order."

*

Alpha dismissed him for the evening, and Fer stalked all the way back to his apartment. An order, he sulked, hunkering down against the wind. Why did he have to make it an order?

Why? Because Alpha knew as well as he did, unless it was an order, he wouldn't do jack shit. In the distance, he saw thunderheads billowing dark and angry and heard the far-off rumble of a storm. He picked up his pace not wanting to add insult to injury by getting caught in a downpour.

He got to his apartment building just as the first drops of rain hit the pavement. By the time he reached his door, rain was coming in sheets. Fer sank onto his sofa and called up the software icon on his HUD. The icon directed him to an online store to purchase and install the program.

"American Robotics' Professional Language Enhancer," he read the software description. "Makes real time corrections and improvement to problematic and inappropriate language and streamlines speech patterns for more professional blah, blah, blah. Fine. Whatever."

He was just about to start the download when his eyes flicked over to where the install button should have been and saw a buy option instead. "Buy? Alright, alright. I got a few bucks." He called up the price and his eyes bugged. "Six— six hundred fucking dollars?!" Lightning flashed outside followed by a crack of thunder. For a second, he felt like The Count from Sesame Street and almost gave in to the urge to follow it with the character's trademark laugh. Almost. There were more pressing matters at hand, like what kind of asshole spent six hundred bucks on correction software. Then he remembered. "Oh wait, Nix is that kind of asshole." He rolled his eyes and began a wide search for similar software making sure to add "free" to the results filter.

The search produced a list of over two hundred options. Fer went to the first result, an app called Clean Speech Now by Friendly Face Media. He'd never heard of Friendly Face Media and didn't like to install software from companies with which he wasn't familiar. But it had thousands of reviews and averaged out at four and a half stars— and it was free. The free was the big part. Besides, if he installed it and it turned out to suck, he could just as easily uninstall it and move on to the next one.

Fer gave a half blink and the software terms and conditions popped up. He blinked twice and scrolled through the info on his HUD all the way to the bottom, barely registering any of the document. It was all legal bullshit anyway, giving the program permission to make changes to his speech patterns and access his personal drives and processors; it was the same shit every time any synthetic downloaded new software. No one ever read the terms and conditions. Fer gave one final blink and the download started.

A progress bar appeared on his HUD; it looked like a sizable download. Fer checked the time and his schedule. It was 19:00, a good stopping point for his day. Just to be sure, he confirmed he had no commitments for the rest of the evening. He was all good. Satisfied with his lack of plans, Fer went to his room, stripped down to his skivvies, and climbed into bed, opting to sleep through the download and the storm outside.

*

Fer awoke to the sound of a text message coming in on his phone. Then another. And another. His systems snapped back online, and he saw the download was complete. Another text. He got up and crossed the room to the bookshelf where his phone lay on its charging pad.

Sunlight streamed through the cracks in his blinds, and he opened them, letting the morning light illuminate the room. He picked up the phone and saw a series of funny cat pictures Anjiko had text to him all in rapid succession. He was about to complain to the void about his scrapper's obsession with cat memes, but decided getting them sent to his phone was much better than when she would send them to his HUD. There was nothing more annoying than being in the middle of a debriefing and suddenly seeing a cat wearing an orange peel on its head like a helmet.

Another text chimed on the screen. "Hot stuff, Anjiko, calm the fun down," he muttered and went to grab some clean shorts from his dresser. He took all of two steps toward the bathroom when he stopped dead.

Hot stuff? That's not what he wanted to say, but sure, fine. His new software was designed to curb his swearing, and that's what it did. It was weird, but he was probably just getting used to it.

Another text alert sounded. "Jelly fudging doughnuts!" he snapped at the phone. "Will you please—" he stopped again and looked worried. "Jelly what?" He repeated the words and decided to do a little test. He thought hard about the word 'fuck,' opened his mouth, and "Fudge." He shook his head. "Flip. Frik. Fark. Fonk." He blinked a few times in rapid succession. "Fonk?" He furrowed his brows. "What kind of moronic smither-biscuit says fonk?" He paused and looked even more confused, "Smither-biscuit? Yeah, no. This isn't gonna work." He brought up the file on his HUD and went to uninstall it, except he couldn't. The button to uninstall the software was grayed out and unable to be accessed.

Fer's eyes darted all over his HUD, opening and reopening the program file. He hoped doing so would somehow make the uninstall option available to him. It did not. A sense of impending doom washed over him. He sat down on the edge of his bed; underwear still clutched in his hand. His eyes were wide and anxious as he stared at that horrible dead button. "Egad. I'm in trouble."

*

Trouble or not, he still had a job to do and today was no different. He read the texts Anjiko sent after her barrage of cats and was reminded the two of them were supposed to grab coffee together before the morning's briefing.

He got dressed and cleaned up just in time to hear Kiku announce her at his door. He took a deep breath; he could do this. All he had to do was keep quiet and maybe no one would notice. "This is gonna sark," he said, putting on his jacket and straightening his captain's bars in the mirror by the front door. "Oh, come on, I can't even say sark?! And sark's not even a flubbing word!" The AI announced Anjiko a second time, and with a frustrated groan, he opened the door.

"Good morning my Fer-Fer!" Anjiko greeted with a cheery smile. Her big green eyes were bright, and her pink hair fell into precisely arranged layers around her ears.

"Anjiko, come on, we talked about this," Fer said, reminding her now that she was an official Omega; he was her direct officer.

"Oh, right," she corrected herself, her exuberance undaunted. "Good morning, my *Captain* Fer-Fer!"

Fer sighed and smiled. "Close enough." He could never be too hard on Anjiko. It just wasn't in him. "How are you today?"

"I'm good," she bubbled as they exited the building into the damp morning. "Did you hear the storm last night? It was a big one! They said parts of town even lost power."

They started down the sidewalk toward the parking garage with Anjiko still chattering away. Most of the time, her incessant chit-chat would get old quick, especially this early in his day. But today Fer was thankful for it. The more she talked, the less he had to. The most he had to do was acknowledge he was listening, and given the circumstances, he felt he could manage an occasional, "Yeah," or, "No kidding?" as the conversation warranted.

They reached Fer's Jeep and got in. Anjiko made sure to point out how it smelled like an ashtray inside, and how something like that would hurt its resale value. He knew that was her not so subtle way of telling him he needed to stop smoking, but the joke was on her because Fer had no intention of selling his Jeep any time soon, or ever.

*

It wasn't until they reached the base Starbucks that Anjiko finally ran out of things to say. In the short time since she arrived at Fer's apartment (which was just two floors below hers) her topics of conversation had run the gamut from how bad last night's storm was, to how her snake, Mr. Slithery Dee, had just shed his skin again, ending with the scholarly reflection of "…so yeah, I guess to a stomach, all potatoes are mashed potatoes. Fer—er, Captain? Are you okay? You seem extra quiet today."

Fer blinked a couple times, having zoned out about five minutes into the conversation. He was still back with Mr. Slithery Dee and his skin. "I'm fine," he said. "Just not feeling chatty today, I guess."

The door under the bright green awning slid open. Inside was a cacophony of blenders, grinders, and mixed banter punctuated with the overwhelming smell of coffee. They passed a few easy chairs where other customers were eyeball deep in their devices, looking up only to sip at their beverages or take a bite of a bagel. They got into the line that was about eight customers deep and waited. After waxing philosophical about potatoes, Anjiko seemed to have run out of things about which to talk, and that was okay. Silence was also good, but Fer was getting anxious. He tended to avoid Starbucks— not that he had a problem with it or anything. The coffee was decent and sometimes they had those chocolate-filled croissants he liked. It was the crowds and the lines he disliked. He didn't begrudge the patrons, though. Starbucks was the only actual coffee shop on base, and people flocked to it like sinners to church. Anything to avoid the coffee in the mess. But, today of all days, he was already on edge. Waiting in the endless line of civilian staff ordering half-caf this or triple-shot that with the extra pump of sugar syrup just made him even more paranoid.

When he and Anjiko made it to the front of the line, they placed their orders with the Jane at the counter and paid. Fer was never so happy to have a cup of coffee in his life. Drinking, like letting Anjiko ramble, meant not talking. Not talking meant not swearing and triggering that two-bit piece of garbage software.

They were about to leave when Anjiko took a sip from her cup and pulled a face.

"What's wrong?" he asked.

"They messed up my order. I ordered a mocha latte; this is chai." She looked at her cup disappointed.

"We've got time; go back and have them fix you a new drink," Fer suggested.

Anjiko looked at the line. It had doubled in length since their arrival and frowned. "No, it's fine. I can drink this."

Fer shook his head. He had been a victim of messed up drive-thru orders too many times to settle for close enough. "No, you shouldn't have to. It's not what you paid for, so they should fix it."

"Captain, really it's okay."

"No. It's not." He grabbed the cup from her. "Here, let me do it."

Fer approached the counter, cutting the line. Behind him someone who had been talking way too loudly on their phone looked up and gave an annoyed objection. Fer ignored the protest and put the cup on the counter. "Excuse me, my friend ordered a mocha. You gave her the wrong order."

The barista, who was in the middle of helping another customer, stopped and rolled his eyes up at Fer. "Order for Anjiko?" he asked with all the enthusiasm of a dying man.

"Yes."

The barista tapped at his screen, recalling the order. "Nope. No, she didn't. It says chai. Do you want to buy a mocha instead?"

"No." Fer could feel his temper biting at him and did his best to ignore it. He took a deep breath. His words were measured and polite, and each one killed him a little inside. "I would like it very much if you just fixed her order... please."

The barista was neither measured nor polite. "But it's not wrong."

Fer's nostrils flared with a forceful exhale, and he grit his teeth as he struggled to maintain his calm. "Yes, it is."

The barista sighed one of those heavy, customer service sighs, turned his screen and pointed to the digital receipt. "No. It's not. If you want a mocha, get back in line and order one."

Fer glared at the stuck-up coffee jockey and lost all his cool. "As per my email, she did order a mamma jammin' mocha. I heard her, by golly! You must have keyed it in wrong, you ten cent brownie-biting muffin-maker! Now bonking fix it!"

The barista stared blank faced, and Fer saw him fighting against a laugh as the corners of his mouth twitched. After a minute of struggle, he gave in. "Hey," he called back, through fits of laughter. "Can one of you muffin-makers grab this guy's mamma jammin' mocha, by golly?"

Fer squeezed his eyes shut, hating every word that had just come out of his mouth. He should have let Anjiko just deal with the chai, but no, he had to go be the hero and fix it for her. By now the barista, his coworkers, and at least four of the people in line behind him were laughing. One of the bystanders had her phone out, hoping to catch more of his strange anti-tantrum so she could put it all over the internet.

Fer set his jaw and clenched his free hand into a fist, lightly bouncing it off the countertop. Never had he been so embarrassed in his life. He did a quick memory scan to check and yep, this was the worst. It was even worse than the time he lost a bet to Reynolds and had to spend the evening at the range dressed in a pink unicorn costume handing out cupcakes.

"Um, Captain?" Anjiko appeared beside him looking worried. "Are you feeling okay?"

"No," he replied. "No, I am not."

"How about we just go?" she suggested and led him outside, abandoning her replacement mocha.

*

"So, you can't uninstall it?" Anjiko asked as the two of them sat side by side on a metal bench outside. It was still wet with rain from the night before, but Fer didn't seem to care so she didn't care either.

"No. I can't." Fer looked at his coffee cup, dejected.

"Have you tried going straight to the site you downloaded it from and uninstalling it from there?"

"Yes."

"Have you looked in the software settings for anything?"

"Yes. All I found was a contract cancellation option. But I didn't agree to any contract." He sipped his coffee and found he no longer wanted it.

"Well, maybe you should drop by the SRC and let them look at you," she suggested. "I'll go on to the morning briefing and fill Alpha and Ino in on what happened and—"

"No! No, no, no! Don't you breathe a gum-balled word to anyone about this. Promise me, Anjiko. Just... just tell them I started coughing up sludge again."

Anjiko grimaced, "Gross, Sir."

"Yeah, well, like you always say, I smoke too much."

"Then, maybe you should stop."

Fer sighed and tried to redirect her back to the matter at hand. "I'm not— never mind. My point is, just lie to them."

Anjiko shook her pink head, and she looked every bit like the child she once was. "I can't lie; Ino will catch me."

"Fine. Then don't lie. Just tell them I'm at the SRC and that's it."

"But that's not it. She'll know, Fer. Ino always knows." Her eyes grew wide and grave.

"I'm sure you'll figure something out." He got up from the bench.

"Now I better get going. I'll drop you off at Central Ops and head over to the SRC. The sooner I get this fonging thing out of my head the better."

*

Fer had just dropped Anjiko off when Godzilla roared from his pocket. He looked at the caller ID on his dashboard, wondering why Nix was calling him all the way from the Confederated Zone. He hit the accept button on the steering wheel.

"Hey, how's Shoddy Shelley?" Fer greeted then groaned.

From the other end of the line Nix gave an odd laugh, *"Well, **Shitty** Shelley is fine. If I ever get stationed at Shoddy Shelley, I'll let you know. Anyway, Alpha called me yesterday and told me you were going to give ARC's vocabulary modifying software a try. I was just curious as to how you liked it so far."*

"And I'd tell you," he began, wanting nothing more than to just hang up on him, "if I actually had six hundred flipping dollars to drop on a piece of poo like that to begin with."

"Piece of..." Nix trailed off, sounding confused. *"So, you didn't download it."*

Fer huffed, "No, funny-face, I didn't."

"Funny-face? Fer, what did you download?"

"Nothing."

"Come on, we both know that's a load of shit. What did you download?"

"Please refer to the attached spreadsheet." His eyes bugged in frustration, and he slammed his fists against the steering wheel.

"What?"

"Perhaps there was some confusion in our last communication. Allow me to— Ugh!" he growled through his clenched teeth. Substituting swears with nonsense was one thing, but spouting off generic email jargon on top of it? Fer was in hell; or rather, heck, given his current situation. "Fine. I downloaded, you know, a substitute. Are you happy, you nosy fopdoodle?"

"A substitute? Of course you did," Nix sighed. *"Why didn't you just install the software Alpha sent you?"*

"Because, as per my email, it cost six hundred dollars!"

Nix went silent and then very slowly, as though he was piecing together the situation as he spoke, said, *"You know Section reimburses you for stuff like that, right?"*

Fer didn't reply. He was busy making all kinds of obscene gestures at his dashboard, thankful the program at least let him give people the finger.

When Fer didn't reply, Nix continued, *"Oh... oh, wow. You didn't, did you? Don't tell me; you were too cheap to buy the good software, so you downloaded the first free option you found, am I right?"*

Fer still didn't respond. He just drove and fumed. From the other end of the call, he heard what started as a low chuckle; a low chuckle which escalated to full on laughter in about five seconds flat, at which point Fer was almost certain Nix was laughing so hard he was crying. "No, I didn't download the first option I found, vile knave!" This was a lie of course, but he didn't care. Nix could fudge right off.

"Fer, why don't you just uninstall that junk and get the right one?"

"Cussadang it! You think I haven't tried? I can't! It's stuck and won't let me get rid of it."

"Why would you install something you couldn't get rid of?"

"Because, friend-o, I didn't know." Nix's barrage of questions was getting annoying.

"Did you not read the terms of service...friend-o?"

Fer snorted but didn't reply; he didn't want to him the pleasure of a response. Of course he didn't read the terms of service. Although, something in him was wishing he had now.

Nix laughed harder, having deduced an answer from Fer's silence. *"You know, you may give me shit about not being a bookworm, but at least I read the terms of service on the stuff I literally put into my brain."*

"Shut up, Nix."

Nix gave a few more good laughs, followed by a few deep breaths. *"Whew, okay,"* he breathed. *"So, what are you going to do?"*

"Right now, I'm headed to the SRC to see if they can help me out."

"Well, good luck. Let me know how it goes. I'll be in touch."

"The H-E-double-hockey-sticks you will."

Nix stifled another laugh on the other end. *"Oh, no. I don't want to miss any of this. I'll definitely be in touch. Good luck... friend-o."*

*

Fer arrived at the SRC and after he was checked in, he was shown to an exam room where he was made to sit in a chair that looked like something out of an old episode of *Star Trek*. There was a panel attached to one side lined with rows of LEDs, some blinking, some solid, each giving the status of his various operating systems. The chair then fed the information into a series of monitors on the wall beside him where an SRC troubleshooter— in this instance, a human with long black and red braids and a mole the size of a pencil eraser by his eyebrow— reviewed it.

Over the course of thirty minutes, he scanned Fer for viruses, malware, data corruption— the whole nine yards— and found nothing unusual. When he finished, he shuffled him off to another exam room; a standard one with a dampening table, adjustable lights, and shelves of tools. After what seemed like endless waiting, the door slid open with a soft hiss and Paige Bryan stepped inside.

Paige, like all SRC employees, was dressed in dark burgundy scrubs and, for the most part, looked just like a medical professional; except, instead of a stethoscope around her neck, she had a tool belt around her hips. Stethoscopes, after all, aren't of much use on people who don't have hearts.

"Oh great," Fer groaned from his seat on the workbench. "I thought you were supposed to be in school, small mammalian primate."

Paige looked up from her tablet and raised an eyebrow. "Three things: First, it's nice to see you, too. Second, it's summer vacation. And third, I think you mean monkey."

"Of course I do." His voice had a frantic edge to it. "I mean exactly what you said, but I

can't say it. I also can't say frack, shoot, darn, bum, or meanie head."

Paige's head made a slow path up and down, and she looked at her tablet again, "Meanie head, huh?" She tapped the screen a few times. "It says here you're having trouble with your speech processor. Troubleshooting found no anomalies in your scans, yet here you are saying shit like bum, looking like you're about to go insane."

"Yeah, that pretty much sums it up."

Paige gave a confirming nod and suddenly the eighteen-year-old girl in front of him was replaced by her mother— all peering eyes and clinical interrogation. What was it he'd heard it called, science mode? That was it, Paige was in science mode and when she was in science mode, she became her mother. To most, it wouldn't be such a bad thing, but Fer and Anita

Bryan had never gotten along. From day one they just took off on the wrong foot and never managed to fix it. Anita was brilliant and knew more about synthetics than anyone he'd ever met, and she knew it. That level of self-awareness always made Fer nervous, and though he would never outright admit it, when Paige acted like her, it also made him nervous.

"So," Paige scrolled through the report from the troubleshooter. "How about we cut to the chase, and you tell me what kind of junk software you put in your brain." Her voice wasn't quite as brusque and condescending as Anita's always was, but it still wasn't the voice of the young lady he sparred with twice a week and was teaching firearm safety to. This was the voice of a professional who, even though she was barely an adult, knew her field better than most of the veteran staff. And just like her mother, Paige knew how good she was.

He cracked a smile and tried to lighten the mood. "What makes you think I—"

"Speech processors don't just up and decide to censor themselves," Paige interrupted. "And the only other real possibility is you got a really hard knock on the head." She raised her eyebrows and looked at him. "Did you?"

"What? No," he said with a frown. So much for lightening the mood.

"Okay." She took a seat on a rolling chair. After adjusting the height a bit, she scooted toward him, and finally smiled. "So, how about you tell me what you did, Captain Grumpy Pants."

Fer smiled back, relieved. At least for the moment, the ghost of Anita Bryan was taking a back seat, and he was able to talk to his friend. He took a breath and for the third time that day, relayed the story of how he downloaded the software and was unable to uninstall it.

"Okay," Paige nodded, leaning back in the chair. "That was super stupid."

"You think I don't know that already?"

"I'm just making sure we're clear," she teased.

Fer rolled his eyes. "Crystal clear."

"So, let's take a look at this app." She got up and took a sleek looking pair of glasses off the shelf and slipped them on him. The glasses, he saw, were outfitted with multiple sensors and cameras, and as soon as they were on, he felt them synch up with his internal operating systems. "I'm going to access your HUD and take a look at this thing for myself." She rolled across the room to a nearby table and opened a laptop.

"Knock yourself out," Fer said over the sound of Paige's fingers dancing over the keyboard. After a few rounds of *clackity-clackity-clack* from the keys, she pushed the screen of the laptop back, so it was flat on the table. A few seconds later, he felt a strange kind of pressure behind his eyes and saw his HUD materialize in his field of vision of its own accord. At the same time, he also saw an image of his HUD hovering above Paige's laptop screen. He flinched and watched the data and imagery come and go in front of him as Paige dragged and tapped at the images in front of her. It felt wrong sharing his HUD, and as she worked, he felt as though he had the closest thing to a headache a synthetic could experience.

"Just relax; I won't be long," Paige said when she noticed his discomfort. "I know it's not fun, but if you think that's bad, try getting a pelvic exam every year."

"I'll pass, my simian friend."

Paige stifled a laugh and shook her head, "What's the name of the software? Wait, never mind, I found it." She tapped on the icon for Clean Speech Now and opened it up. "Looks like you can cancel your contract right here."

"But I didn't sign a contract. There was nothing ever mentioned."

Paige swiveled around in her chair and Fer saw Anita Bryan staring back at him again. "You saw nothing in the terms of service?" Fer didn't answer. "Because surely, *surely* you understand when you agree to the terms of service it, for all intents and purposes, becomes a contract... right?" Once again, Fer didn't answer. Paige inhaled long and slow and exhaled in much the same manner. She shook her head at him like a disappointed teacher and spun back to her computer. "Sweet Satan in a sauna, Fer. How can you be so cavalier with your own brain?"

"Look, I was ticked off at Alpha. I wasn't thinking. I just wanted—"

"To do the bare minimum to spite him?" she interrupted. "Real mature."

"Hey, I didn't come here for a lecture. Just fix me for Pete's sake."

"Yes, Sir," Paige replied with mock enthusiasm and went back to work.

Fer watched the app's terms of service scroll in front of him as Paige read them. This time he read them too, and by the time she was done, he felt like all his CLC had been replaced with ice water.

"So, I'm sure you've read what I just did, but just in case, allow me to paraphrase: By agreeing to the terms and conditions here, you agreed to keep the software for a twenty-four-hour period. The good news is at the end of the twenty-four hours the software will automatically disable itself.

"But I can't afford to wait a whole donking day!"

"Well, then your only other option is to break the contract," Paige said.

"Great! Let's do it."

Paige held up a hand. "I'm not done. If you break the contract, you will be penalized... You did read the words this time around, right?" Fer gave a noncommittal shrug. Paige sighed. "See, this is why we can't have nice things." She did some quick mental math. "If you cancel early, you're penalized fifty dollars for every hour left on the contract. So, it's been what—"

"About fourteen hours," Fer groaned.

"So, you're looking at a cancellation fee of just around five hundred bucks." She looked at him with equal parts shock and amusement. "You just more or less ransom-wared your brain. Way to go, genius."

Fer felt like he had just been smacked in the teeth with a two-by-four. *"Well, that's it,"* he thought. *"Just scrap me now because there is no barking way I will ever live this down."* He tensed and ran both his hands over his head, dragging his fingers through the short bristles of his hair when he realized even his own thoughts were censored. "How— but— how is this even legal?" he argued. "You can't just get people to pay you to get rid of your bullship software!"

"You can if it's stated in the terms of service, and people agree to them." Paige pressed her lips together and took pity on him. "Look, I agree it's shady as hell, but it's not illegal. Actually, it's a great way to scam cash. Put out a free piece of shit software, hide a cancellation fee in the terms of service, and just wait for some frustrated Jane to cave and fork over the cash." She relinquished control on Fer's HUD, and he felt the pressure in his head vanish.

"But it had tons of reviews; most of them good," he lamented. "I just... ugh." He gave a defeated groan and slumped on the workbench.

"Companies fabricate reviews and pad their ratings all the time. Now, that's illegal, but it still happens." She rolled across the room and put a reassuring hand on his leg. "Look, you screwed up and downloaded something you shouldn't have. It happens. My grandma once wrecked her entire computer because she wanted to download some free screensavers. Luckily, you haven't wrecked your brain."

"No, it's just being held hostage."

"You could always just pay the fee," Paige suggested.

"Like fun I will!" he snapped then thought a minute. "Wait, Nix said Section will reimburse us for junk like this."

Paige shook her head and held up a hand, cutting him off. "Section will reimburse you for business related purchases, not for being a dumbass."

As though on cue, Godzilla roared in Fer's pocket. He groaned again and retrieved his phone.

"What's wrong?" Paige asked.

"Nix is calling to give me more guff over this mess."

"Nix?" Paige perked up. "Gimme the phone! I want to talk to him!" She launched herself out of her chair at Fer, grabbing for his cell. "Gimme, gimme! I haven't talked to him since he was on leave at Christmas!" She was almost climbing on him trying to get at the phone while he held it above his head, out of her reach.

"Will you back off?" Fer snapped, trying, but failing, to push her back with one hand. Paige was almost in his lap, having come dangerously close to kneeing him in the crotch, when the roaring stopped.

"Goddammit," She huffed and sat back down. No sooner than her butt hit her chair, Fer's phone roared again. She beamed. Fer just sighed.

"He's a persistent crashhole, isn't he?" he grumbled and answered the phone. "What?"

"Hey Pumpkin, how's it going?" Nix greeted, his voice dripping with mock sweetness.

"Shut up, frog-face. Now, what do you want?"

"I told you, I'm just keeping in touch to see how your day is going. And from the sound of it, I'm guessing it's not going well."

"Actually, I'm at the SRC and Paige is trying to fix me."

"Glad to hear it. Tell Miss Bryan I said hi."

"Tell her yourself, she's right here."

Fer lowered the phone, hit the speaker, and held it out to Paige who was just beside herself with giddiness.

"Hey Nix," she beamed and waved at the phone, even though it wasn't a video call.

"Good morning, Miss Bryan," he said. *"How have you been?"*

"I'm good. Just trying to fix Fer. Although, there's not much of anything to fix. He can either fork over half a grand to uninstall the software or wait it out for ten more hours."

"*Oh?*"

"Yeah, he basically let his brain be taken hostage. You know what he did, right?"

Nix let out a long, contented sigh. *"Aah, my day just keeps getting better and better. Has he lost his temper on you yet? Have you heard it in action?"*

"Yep, sure have, by gosh and by gum," she said, mimicking Fer's censored vocabulary.

"What does he plan on doing?"

"He plans on hanging up on you if you don't lay off, you pizzle-brained rapscallion," Fer interrupted. "The only reason I haven't yet is because Diddy Kong here looked like she was going to explode if she didn't get to talk to you."

"What? We miss you," Paige shrugged.

"*She* misses you." Fer grunted.

"Alas, it's true," she agreed.

"I miss you too, Miss Bryan. But I do have to go. Chin up, Fer. Remember, you could always just, you know not..." he stifled a laugh. *"Not swear."* He tried again to curb his laughter, caught his breath, and continued. *"I'm sorry, I can't even think that with a straight face, let alone say it. Anyway, it was nice talking to you, Miss Bryan. Fer, I'll be in touch."*

"Aaw, don't go!" Paige protested.

"Normally I'd love to chat, but it's coffee day, and I'd hate to miss a minute of it. Take care." His voice trailed off, and they heard him greet someone named Patrick before they each gave a simultaneous sendoff of, "Enjoy your coffee," and, "Smurf you."

The two sat in the exam room looking at each other for a minute.

"Are you happy?" Fer asked Paige who was still looking smitten.

"Yes," she said, her smile still stretching from ear to ear.

"Shall I send an orderly to fetch you some new panties?" he teased.

Paige's eyes went wide, and she swatted him on the shoulder. "Fer! That is grossly inappropriate banter!" Then she lightened up and grinned back. "I can fetch my own panties, thank you."

They both laughed; Paige's attraction to Nix was pretty much legendary among most of her friends and colleagues, and she always took the teasing in stride.

"So, what do I do?" Fer asked once the moment had passed.

Paige hopped up onto the workbench beside him and bobbed her head side to side, weighing the options. "Well, you could pay the fee and cancel the contract."

"Not gonna happen. I don't just have five hundred bucks to drop."

"Okay. Then you just have to wait it out."

Fer moaned and put his head in his hands. "That's ten hours."

"Or, third option, I could give you the money," Paige suggested.

"No. Absolutely not," he said through his fingers. "First rule of friendship is you never borrow or loan money between each other."

"But that's dumb. It's not like I need the cash. Mom and Dad left me with more than enough. When you combine that with my paychecks from here and the fact I don't have to pay rent or bills yet, I can afford to—"

"No. I'm not taking your money. End of discussion."

"Then, I guess your only option is to wait it out."

"Seems that way."

Paige shifted on the workbench and the paper liner beneath them crinkled as she moved. "If you want my advice, just take the rest of the day off. Go home, go to sleep, or watch TV or whatever until the contract expires." She patted his shoulder. "Sorry I can't help you more."

Fer shook his head, "No, you did as much as you could. This is my funk up. I guess I have to live with it."

"Atta boy." She hopped off the workbench and tapped at her tablet. "I'll have your discharge papers filed in just a second. You're good to go."

*

Fer left the SRC and called up his schedule on his HUD. He'd already missed the morning briefing and hoped Anjiko managed not to cave and spill the beans to Alpha and Ino. Judging from the lack of angry messages from Alpha, it was safe to say she succeeded in keeping his secret. He had some things he needed to do, but nothing he couldn't postpone a day with an email. He blinked open his inbox and sent a generic notification out to whoever needed it and headed back to his apartment.

Upon his arrival home, he decided to take Paige's advice and just watch some TV until the contract expired. He flipped through the guide and found an *Ice Shark* marathon on one of the twenty-four-hour movie channels. The *Ice Shark* movies weren't good by any stretch, but they were entertaining enough, and there were a lot of them. It was the perfect way to let his brain shut off and run the clock out.

Fer hadn't had a day off in who knows how long, and he was more than happy to reacquaint himself with the subtle art of binge-watching TV. Other than a call from Nix every hour on the hour, it was turning out to be a nice way to spend a day. Nix was easy enough to deal with, anyway. Fer figured he'd just as soon humor the poor, bored Major as opposed to resisting. Each time Godzilla roared, Fer would pick up the phone, rattle off half a dozen failed swears, then hang up to the sound of unbridled laughter on the other end. He considered it his good deed for the day.

*

It was somewhere in the middle of *Ice Shark 4* that his cell rang again. It rang, not roared. Fer reached across the sofa and grabbed the phone from the end table. It was Chief Walker.

"Yeah, Chief," he greeted.

"Captain, I've got a pretty heated situation here in town and could use your help."

Fer looked at the time. He still had forty-five minutes before the contract expired. So close, yet so far away. "Chief Walker, this isn't really a good time. Is there any way I can send one of my scrappers in my place?"

He heard her sigh. *"If it were any other day, I'd say okay, but I was told to call you,*

specifically."

"Oh, you were, huh?" This piqued Fer's interest.

"I'm not happy about it either, Captain," Chief Walker huffed. *"But my witness is insistent that if anyone can deescalate this, it's you."*

Fer frowned; unsure just how effective he could be at the moment. The incident at Starbucks earlier that day coupled with Nix's phone calls didn't just annoy him, they messed with his confidence. So much of his effectiveness as a scrapper was built on him being mean and intimidating. He found he couldn't be either of those saying things like pillow-fluffer, and heavens to Betsy. But, on the other hand, he knew if he didn't go, he'd be right back in Alpha's office again getting another stern dad lecture; this time for blowing off a call for aid. "Okay, Chief. Send me the address, I'm on my way." Compromised speech or no, he had work to do.

*

Fer arrived at the specified address and showed his ID to the officer at the far end of the blockade. The officer deactivated the bright red barrier spanning the street and let Fer drive through to the scene. As soon as he parked his Jeep and got out, he knew right then why he was called. The disturbance was coming from The Olive Branch, an all-Jane restaurant run by his longtime friend, Jet. He saw three squad cars and a group of officers surrounding the building, weapons drawn. Across the street, behind the blockades, about two dozen civilians all came out of the woodwork to gawk at the scene.

"Captain Fer."

Fer looked to his right and saw Chief Walker approach with Jet close behind. Her boots fell heavy and fast against the pavement, and the high evening sun glared off her badge. Her dark hair was pulled back into a tight ponytail and tucked up into her hat, making her already sharp features seem sharper.

"What the blazes is this, Chief?" Fer asked.

"We've got a bit of a hostage situation, unfortunately," she said in a tone that was all business. "Three humans are being held inside. At least one needs medical attention."

"Is it a corruption?"

She shook her head. "No. But the Jane inside is about as hostile as one."

"Have your officers tried to engage the suspect?"

"Of course not. Synthetics are your jurisdiction."

Fer nodded and turned to Jet. "How the heck did this happen?"

Jet rubbed the back of his neck with one big hand and frowned. "It was all so fast, to be honest. Things were going just like any other day when I got this group of three college kids coming in off the street." Humans weren't unwelcome at Jet's place, but beyond Paige, they were a rarity. "It took 'em a minute to realize my place isn't their typical college hang out, but you know me, I'm never one to discriminate, so I let them know they were welcome and grabbed them some menus." He paused and looked back toward the restaurant. "That's when one of the guys at the bar gets up and loses his shit."

"Anyone I know?" Fer asked.

Jet shook his head and rubbed at an old, faded marinara stain on his apron. "He's only been coming around for the last couple weeks. I don't think you've ever seen him. His name's Lux— big guy; I mean big. Shiraz just calls him Two-Ton McScary."

Fer looked over to Shiraz, who was lingering behind Jet, and saw her with her arms out to the side, puffing herself up, miming how big the guy was.

"Okay, okay, so Two-Ton loses his doo-doo on what? The humans?" He pursed his lips and screamed internally when he heard the word 'doo-doo' come out of his mouth. Judging by the confusion on Jet's face, he caught it too.

"Um, yeah. He did. He started in on how this was the only place in town he could get away from humans, and he intended to keep it that way. Being the owner, I told him to lay off or get out. You know me, I like humans for the most part— hell one of my favorite customers is a human, and I think we both know who I mean." Fer nodded, and Jet continued, "Anyway, he said he didn't plan on doing either and went on some tirade about how Janes need more places catered to them and blah, blah, blah— and yeah maybe he's right, but that's neither here nor there. Then he stood up and chucked his barstool at the kids and knocked one of 'em out cold. After that, the humans called 911. The cops showed up, and I told Chief Walker here to call you."

Fer nodded, picking his way through Jet's statement, separating the actual information from the filler his friend was so good at padding his stories with. "Are they still inside?"

"Yep, most of the other customers bolted as soon as Lux tossed the barstool. He told me to leave, or he'd clock another one of them, so I did. Once I was out, he locked himself inside."

"Is he armed— I mean with anything other than a barstool?"

"Not that I can tell."

"We just need to get inside so the paramedics can tend to the injured hostage, but we can't do that with him in there," Chief Walker said.

"So, you need me to take him out?"

"Preferably without further casualties."

Fer nodded. "Okay, let me see what I can do." He approached the door to Jet's and rapped on the glass. "Hey, Two-Ton McScary! This is Captain Fer from The Section for Corruption Prevention and Research. How about—"

An angry voice boomed from inside, cutting him off. "I'm not corrupted, Captain! Go home!"

"Maybe not," Fer agreed. "But you're acting like you are, so I've been called in to either talk some sense into you or kick your hiney— er… bottom— ugh! Beat you up!"

"Oh yeah? You're gonna kick my hiney, huh? Let me tell you something—"

"No, let me tell *you* something, kitten whiskers!" Fer cringed. His internal screaming was about to become external screaming with every word, but he soldiered on. "You've got a human in there in need of gosh darn medical care, so you can either let the paramedics in to help them, or I'll smash this heckin' door down with my bare mother-hugging hands. Got me, snickerdoodle?" He winced and banged his head against the door in aggravation.

"Oh, I got you alright," Lux said after taking a few seconds to process Fer's threat. "You're a fucking lunatic! What the hell is wrong with you?" It was clear Lux was about as intimidated by Fer as a T-rex would be by a basket of puppies. In fact, the Jane inside Jet's restaurant seemed to think Fer was crazy or, at the very least, a total joke. "Hey, cop-lady!" Lux shouted. "Did you get this guy off the recall line or something? Get him outta here! I'm not negotiating with busted hardware."

The next thing Fer knew, Chief walker had him by the arm and was dragging him away from the restaurant.

"Captain! What on earth is wrong with you? Do you think this is funny?" She demanded.

Frustration and anger coursed through Fer, inferno hot. He glared down at Chief Walker so hard it almost looked like he was trying to ignite her with his eyes like Superman on the verge of a temper tantrum.

"No, Chief, I don't think this is funny, dadgummit! I think it's pretty flimflamming awful, but someone had to complain to my biscuit-baking boss about my language being too doinking inappropriate! So now I have this glob-slobbing software stuck in my head that makes me sound like a demented evangelical housewife! That is what is wrong with me, and no, I don't find it fucking funny!" Fer stopped short; his eyes went wide. "I don't find it fucking funny," he said again, quieter. He checked the time. His HUD read 19:00. The contract had expired, and just like Paige said, the software disabled itself. He gave a single relieved laugh. "Fuck. Fuck! I can say fuck!" He looked at Chief Walker and Jet. "Fuck, shit, damn, hell, ass, cock— I'm free… Holy shit, I'm free!" Relief washed over him like a hot shower, and he felt the weight of the last twenty-four hours vanish down the drain.

"Fine, great, you're free," Chief Walker said, more annoyed than anything, interrupting his reverie. "Now, can you please do what I called you here for?"

Fer was about to bolt back to the restaurant and get to work— *really* get to work— then stopped short, remembering what happened the last time he and the Chief worked together. "If I do, am I going to find myself in the principal's office again?" he asked.

Chief Walker grunted and crossed her arms. "Look, I got upset and called Alpha last time because I don't know you well enough to discern between Captain Fer being Captain Fer and raw synthetic anger— which, frankly, scares the devil out of me. I respect synthetics like you as people equal to myself, but I also know your kind can liquefy me if I wind up on the business end of your tempers." She gave a solemn nod. "That's how I lost my cousin. He and his fellow officers were sent after that psycho Joshua." She trailed off for a second. "And I'm sure we all remember how well that went."

Fer nodded his agreement and sympathy. He remembered that night. Nix yelling into his phone to call off the cops only to be too late. He recalled the massacre that greeted them at the cabin, and how he and his squadmates barely made it out alive themselves; Nix lost an arm, Ino went blind, and he got stabbed in the leg.

"That's fair," he said at last. "I'm sorry. I didn't know."

"It's okay," Chief Walker replied. "You do now." She folded her arms over her chest and sighed, "Listen, if it's going to be that big of an issue, use your trashy language. Be scary and angry, but just don't do it to my officers or myself. Like I said, I respect you, but I also expect the same in return. Can we at least agree to that?"

"Yes," Fer replied without hesitation. "Yes. I can do that."

"Good," Chief Walker said, and for the first time in their short relationship, smiled at him. "Now, go get 'im."

Fer sprinted back to the door, raised his boot, and kicked it clean off its hinges. "Hey, asshole, you're fucked now!"

Of Love and Lattes

It's Tuesday which, in my world, is latte day. I normally don't do the whole eating and drinking thing, but Fer got me drinking coffee just before I left for the Confederated Zone, and well, it kind of stuck. Granted, according to him, I don't drink 'real' coffee which is to say a cup of sludge so black and strong you can stand a spoon in it. No, I prefer to have my coffee in a somewhat more refined manner.

I enter the Thanks-A-Latte coffee shop at the corner of 3rd and Jordan and place my usual order: a double latte to go. It's nothing fancy but still elegant in its simplicity. As I wait, I look at the art hanging on the walls. It's all stuff from the university art students and it's pretty good, except all the paintings are done in the same style. I know there are at least three different artists being featured on these walls, but all their stuff looks the same. It's like the school only teaches one way to paint. It's bland. It's boring.

"Nick," The barista calls and looks my way.

"It's Nix," I correct…again… and pick up my drink. I head toward the door and stop to pop the lid off my cup. I know what I'm going to see, or rather, what I'm not going to see. I stare down at the plain, white topping of milk foam and sigh. It's the one and only time I miss the Confederated Zone.

*

One year earlier - Columbia, Missouri

I push the door open to Impresso Espresso knowing today is going to be different. I've been coming to this shop every Tuesday and Thursday for the last year of my almost three-year tour here at Fort Shelley. There aren't many small shops still open, what with the fighting as bad as it is.

The Eastern US has had a controlling presence in the Confederated Zone ever since the second civil war. It doesn't belong to the EUS, but the powers that be act like it does so they can take advantage of the shipping routes along the Mississippi River. In return, we try to offer much needed aid to the people here— and that includes a Section presence.

There aren't many synthetics actually living in the CZ, but it is frequented by refugees coming East, mostly from the Western US, and Texas. The Confederated citizens often don't know what to make of us and prefer to keep their distance. They're not hostile, but they definitely don't trust us. I can somewhat understand why. The refugees who pass through here are often tired, damaged, and desperate, and sometimes desperate people do desperate things. That's where my Scrappers at Fort Shelley and I come in. We help keep the peace between the humans and synthetics.

Unfortunately, refugees aren't the only thing keeping me busy over here. I wish they were the worst of my problems, but no such luck. The Western US has been trying to get a foothold here and take over ever since the former US split up. They want that river just as much as we do. Up until recently, it's just been little skirmishes here and there, but two years ago, the West launched an invasion, and ever since, the CZ has been a full-on war zone as the Eastern Army, along with the Confederated National Guard, try to hold them off.

People's lives have been upended. Families have been torn apart; homes and schools destroyed. A lot of businesses have been shuttered to hold off looters because it's not just synthetic refugees trying to get East now. Thousands of Confederated citizens are fleeing. The EUS government is trying to relocate as many people as they can, in as organized a manner as they can, but the process is long, and most won't wait. Most just pack their things and go, opting to let Eastern border patrol figure it out for them.

Luckily, Patrick is still hanging in there. I'm glad. He makes this whole tour bearable. More than bearable. He makes it enjoyable. He's the owner of this fine little establishment, and he also makes a mean latte. He's soft-spoken, educated, and genuinely cares about his community of customers and fellow business owners. But I'll be honest, I stopped coming here for the coffee a long time ago.

I look around the shop, and see that it's empty which, even in these circumstances, is unusual. Normally, there are at least a couple customers along with Chunhua, his one and only employee. The bell on the door jingles as it closes behind me, and it makes me smile.

The walls around me are covered in paintings— all Patrick's work. His style is different than mine. His work is all about mood and emotion, whereas I like technical things like light and shadow and depth of feel, but it speaks to me all the same. I could spend hours staring at these paintings. I even bought one a few months ago. Patrick was so thrilled to have sold one I didn't think he'd ever stop smiling.

I approach the counter and see Patrick, his dark hair perfectly combed as always, dressed in an immaculate white button-down shirt and brown apron. It's the only outfit I've ever seen him in. If I hadn't been designed to remember every face I ever see, I seriously don't think I'd be able to recognize him wearing anything else. The sleeves of his shirt are rolled up to his elbows and he's already tamping down ground espresso beans for me. He looks up, and his usual welcoming grin is tinged with sadness.

"Hey, Major Blue-eyes," he greets me and coaxes the portafilter into place on the machine.

"Good morning, Patrick. How's my favorite barista today?" I ask and get comfortable against the counter, or at least I try. Today is different. Today I'm not comfortable. My chest feels like I have a brick lodged inside it, and it's hard to not let my discomfort show.

"I hope I'm your only barista," Patrick replies with a raised eyebrow, trying to lighten the mood. "Have you been drinking around behind my back?"

I snap out of my gloom for a moment and laugh. "I'd never dream of it. And just because you're my only barista doesn't lessen the fact that you're my favorite." I shift against the counter and feel something jab me in the side. I pull the book out of the inner pocket of my jacket and put it down on the counter. It's an old paperback with the title *Old Man's War* in bold, yellow letters on the cover. Patrick insisted I read it and let me borrow it last week when I returned his copy of *Kitchen Confidential*—which was good. This one, however, Patrick said was his absolute favorite, and I can tell. The sharpness of the book's corners has been blunted with age and use, and it's been read so many times, the spine is starting to split down the middle. Patrick looks at the book then up at me.

"You finished it already?" he asks, surprised.

"I did," I say, then smile when I think of the full-on breakdown Fer would have over this.

"What's so funny?"

"Nothing," I reply. "Just that back home I'm not exactly known for being well-read." I push the book across the counter toward him.

"No, you keep it," he says, putting his hand over mine.

As he pushes the book back toward me, I feel his fingers tighten around my hand. I wait for him to flinch or recoil because my skyn doesn't feel exactly like his, but he doesn't. He never does. He just looks at me with his soft eyes and says, "You can give it back to me later."

Later.

Who knows when later will be? Next year when my tour here is up? Or in another four if General Keith decides to extend it? Later could be any time. What if something happens and later never gets here?

"Patrick, I don't—"

"Did you enjoy it?" he interrupts and places his other hand on top of mine, pressing it firmly onto the book.

"Yes," I tell him. And it's true. I really did. Its themes of friendship, personal identity, and what makes one human struck a key with me. Also, it was just an overall good story. "Yes, of course. I spent every bit of down time I had reading it."

"Then read it again." Patrick's voice is warm but sad. "Read it again and get it back to me whenever you can."

I know this is just his way of ensuring we see each other again, so I concede. "Okay. I'll hang on to it. But, just for the record, I don't need a reason to want to see you. When all this is over, we'll—"

"I know," he smiles and lets my hand go. Then he adds on, "But it never hurts to have a little insurance."

I nod and chuckle as Patrick gets back to making my coffee. As he works, I look around the shop again trying to be casual, but probably failing. I've never been good at things like this. To my defense, I've also never been in this position before. I know we'll have to address the elephant in the room sooner or later, but I just can't bring myself to do it, so instead I ask, "Where's Chunhua and all your regulars? It's not like the shop to be this empty." Even though I know damn well why the shop is empty.

Patrick nods at my stunning skills of observation and pours some milk into a little metal pitcher. "Yesterday was my last day," he says. "Technically, I'm closed right now."

The statement registers, but it's lost to the sound of the steamer as it screams to life. We don't speak as he steams the milk. Mostly because it's loud but also because I don't know what to say. I stand at the counter and fidget with one of the wooden stir-sticks from the plastic dispenser. I knew this day was coming. I'd been preparing for it. Hell, I'm the one who made it happen. This is a good thing. I shouldn't be sad right now, but I am.

The steamer calms to a soft hiss then fizzles out. Patrick gets to work pouring the milk over the espresso. I watch him twist and turn the pitcher letting just the right amount of foam or milk pour as he needs it. He is an artist in every sense. As he works, he tells me, "The only reason I'm open today is so I can…" he takes a long, slow breath. A difficult breath. The kind you take when you're trying to keep your emotions from getting the better of you. "Well, I wanted to make your coffee and say goodbye."

Goodbye.

The word hits me hard, and I grimace at the sound of it. I don't want to hear this word. I don't want to say it. But this is the bed I've made. I'd rather lose him here for a little while than have him stay and be in constant danger of being lost forever.

He hands me the ceramic cup. As I take it, my fingers touch his and we stay like that for a moment. Then the moment passes, and as I always do, I look at the work of art crafted in the foam. Today it's a rose. I stare at it for a long moment and smile.

"Sorry it's not a real one," Patrick says.

"I like this one better," I reply.

We both smile at each other, and I take a seat at my usual table. A minute or two later, Patrick joins me with his own coffee.

After my first couple weeks of coming here, Patrick and I hit it off making small talk at the counter. At first, I think he was just interested in the novelty of someone like me coming into his shop. I can't fault his curiosity; synthetics are a rare sight in places like the CZ, and we Janes are even rarer still. Granted, lately that seems to be changing, but it's nothing like back home.

Eventually, my novelty wore, off and it evolved into something a little more personal. After he finished fixing my latte, he'd take his fifteen-minute break and join me at my table where we'd talk about... well, just about everything.

It wasn't long after, I noticed he was stretching his breaks out an extra minute or two until Chunhua caught on and offered to manage things while Patrick had his 'little coffee date.' I also found myself making up excuses to stay longer. I know, I know, it's terrible of me to shirk my duties as a Section officer, but I don't care. It's not like I blew off anything serious. Come on, I'm not Fer.

It was during these conversations that I learned this shop wasn't his, but his late husband, Carson's. Patrick told me, on one particularly slow afternoon, how Carson was killed six years ago in one of those little skirmishes with the West I mentioned earlier. There was a storm that day, and as he told me about it, we watched the rain outside. I can tell Patrick still misses him. Just a few weeks ago, we sat at this same table and quietly shared a piece of cake to celebrate what would have been his forty-fifth birthday. Like I said, I normally don't like to do the whole eating and drinking thing unless I have to, but in that instance, I was happy to make an exception.

After Carson was killed, Patrick left his position as an art professor at the University of Missouri to keep the shop running. Even though he loves what he does, he misses being able to paint every day. Most of the stuff on the walls here is pretty old, back from his teaching days.

Don't get me wrong. It wasn't all dead spouses and missing our hobbies. We'd also talk about happier things. He'd tell me about the books he was reading, and after dealing with my blank-faced 'I've never read it' replies for weeks on end, challenged me to read *The Hobbit*. I leapt at this, not only because he asked me to, but because I recall, very clearly, Jake Bryan harassing me to the point of abject embarrassment about it.

I told him things too, mind you. I told him all about Alpha and my little makeshift family back home. I told him all about the Joshua incident a few years back and how we lost some very good people because of him. On another particularly slow day, I told him the story of the Black Friday Riots and how I found Anita Bryan, amid the rubble and held her as she died. That was a hard one. I'd never told anyone that story, not even Alpha. But, on the other end of the spectrum, I very much enjoyed telling him all about Fer downloading some crap software that messed up his ability to swear. I may have even put him on speakerphone once so Patrick could listen in when I called him. We laughed until we both thought we'd pass out. Chunhua had to come check on us to see if we were okay.

But our favorite topic of conversation is art and painting. We could probably spend entire afternoons discussing different techniques and sharing our work. I showed him some of the photos I had of my paintings on my phone, and you'd have thought he was looking at the Mona Lisa— I was flattered.

Sometimes, when he was working, I'd catch him looking at me from across the shop, and I knew he wasn't just gawking at the Mechanical Man like everyone else.

"So, what next?" I ask and sip my drink. I try and keep my tone hopeful and upbeat, but it's hard.

"Well," Patrick sighs and looks around. "The papers were all cleared yesterday. After I lock up here, I'll load up my stuff, grab Mom and Sasha, and head for New York. They're finishing up the last-minute packing right now. This time next week, we'll be relocated out of here."

"That's good," I say.

Patrick's voice grows distant and thoughtful. "We applied for relocation assistance only six months ago—"

"And you've been waiting for six months too long," I cut him off. I know where this is going.

"Others have been waiting much longer," he tells me in his even, gentle voice. "I'm not saying we're not grateful, Nix, it just seems… wrong."

"It's not wrong to know people with connections," I tell him, annoyed at his objection, mild as it is. I know I shouldn't be. I also know I did pull some— okay, a lot— of strings to fast track his paperwork. "You can't just expect me to stand by and let you and your family live in a warzone. Not when I can do something about it."

Patrick reaches across the table and takes my hand again. His dark eyes are warm and patient. "When we met, I wasn't expecting…" he trails off as his words fail him. "What I mean to say is, when I decided to get to know you, it wasn't because of your connections." He squeezes my hand and grins, "It was those big blue eyes of yours." We both laugh. "Honestly. They are criminally gorgeous. How do you live with yourself?"

I laugh a little and shrug. "I don't know, avoid mirrors, I guess?"

We laugh again, but it's a little forced. We're nearing the end of our conversation, and we both know it. After a moment, Patrick looks down at our hands and then back up at me. "You didn't have to save us."

"I know," I tell him. "But I wanted to."

He takes a long, slow breath. He seems relieved, like he's come to terms with what's happening and feels less guilty about it.

"Thank you," he says. "It'll be nice to sleep easy again, not worrying about whether a bomb's going to go off outside the apartment or shop. It'll be good to get Sasha back in school again, too."

We're both ignoring our coffees, not wanting to let each other's hands go.

"I wish I could've met her," I say. Sasha being Patrick's eight-year-old daughter.

"Me too. And you will once this is all over." He falters for a second. "I mean, if you still want to."

"Of course I'll still want to. I have a book to return, remember? We just had a whole conversation about it," I joke, already imagining our reunion. "What about the shop?"

We both look around the empty cafe and the finality of the situation settles in.

"Board it up, I guess, and hope it's still here if we ever get to come home. I asked Chunhua if she wanted it, but she said not only no, but hell no."

"You're just going to leave all this equipment?"

He laughs and looks at me like I've just asked him if the sky was blue or if bombs went boom. "Well, I can't take it with me. I don't even know my new address yet. And even if I did, this isn't a 'hire movers and take it all with you' situation."

I sigh. "I know, it just seems a shame to leave it."

"It is, but it's fine. Once I get settled, I'll get new stuff."

"Or I could—"

"No," he cuts me off. "We'll be fine. If my mom and grandparents could walk all the way here from Honduras with nothing but a few backpacks between them, I can fly a few hours to New York and get a new espresso machine when I arrive."

I nod. He's got a point. "You know, it's funny," I say, somewhat changing the subject. "I'm originally from New York."

"You are?" he replies. "You never told me."

"Well, I don't remember it, so I don't ever talk about it. I actually don't remember anything before Section. I just know Alpha told me he found me in New York with no name, no Synthetic Registration Number, no memory, nothing. It's why they call me Nix. I had zero, nada, nix."

"Well, maybe you can visit sometime when this is over. Perhaps it will jog your memory." He lets me go and takes a long sip from his cup. When he's done, he wipes the foam moustache off his upper lip with a napkin. He sits the cup down, reaches across the table and takes my hand again. He squeezes it and runs his thumb against my knuckles. "You know, I never said it before, but you're warmer than I thought you'd be," he says. "I grew up familiar with synthetics, but I only knew about Janes from the internet or TV. To us out here, a Jane is like a Jedi. You hear all about them, and you know they exist somewhere, but the chances of actually seeing one in real life are slim to none."

I nod, understanding the *Star Wars* reference, but only because Paige schooled me in it a while back during one of her 'how the hell do you not know this' tirades. I smile and give him leave to continue. "The next thing I know, I've got one visiting my shop twice a week for an entire year." I reach up and touch his cheek. He nuzzles against my hand, and I can feel the scruff of his goatee against my palm. "You're nothing like I expected."

"Neither are you," I smile.

We sit there in silence unsure what to do; both knowing but resisting the inevitability of our parting. Finally, Patrick gets up. He picks up both our cups and heads back behind the counter. "This one's probably gone cold. Let me make you a fresh one for the road." And I let him. How could I not?

"You've got all my contact information, right?" I ask.

"I do."

"You can email me any time. And I'll call whenever I get a chance."

"I know you will."

We both nod as though putting the final details in a big, dangerous plan.

"There's one more thing," I say. "I want you to do something for me."

"Anything," he replies, and I know he's sincere.

"I want you to start painting again. Not...not like right now or anything... th- that would be stupid. But you know... When... when you get settled." It's almost time to go. I'm falling all over my words now and I can't stop it. "Looking at your work has been like looking at pieces of home." I see his face redden. He always blushes when people compliment his art. "You're an amazing artist. This war has taken so much from you, don't let it take that, too." I force my lips to smile, and I see Patrick do the same.

"I will," he nods, in a way that's too fast to be casual. "And when I do, I'll think of you, my Major Blue-Eyes."

As he hands me the cup, he leans across the counter and plants a kiss on my lips. I'm caught off guard but only for a second. I've been kissed before, but this time it's different. This time it's... real. I can't think of a better word for it than that. It's real. As soon as the initial shock wears off, I try to lean into him, but it's too late. He's already pulled away, and I'm left at the counter holding my latte like an idiot. I feel like I'm dying inside, and at the same time, I feel more alive than ever. I look at Patrick and there are tears in his eyes.

"Be safe out there," he tells me. "And keep my book safe."

I nod. "I will." I start to back away from the counter. "Have a safe trip. I..."

"No," Patrick says, smiling through tears. "Don't. I know what you're going to say, but don't." We stare at each other for a long moment. "Because if you finish that sentence, then it's out there, and it's a real thing, and then I'll have to lock that door and take you East with me, and we both know that can't happen."

I nod again and chance a smile. "I wouldn't mind that."

"I know. But kidnapping is a crime, and jail is real." Even now he's trying to make a joke.

I give him one last smile then finally say the words I've been dreading.

"Goodbye, Patrick. I'll see you again." I turn and make my way out the door as fast as I can. I don't glance back, as much as I want to. I know if I do, I'll turn around and go right back. And I can't. So, I keep moving, willing one foot in front of the other.

As I walk, I pop the lid off my latte and look at the simple foam heart. I stare at it and start to feel the heaviness in my chest again. The sadness accompanying it is crushing. This hurts in a way I've never experienced before, and I don't know how to make it stop. I realize, after a second, that I'm crying. I can't remember the last time I cried. Jake and Anita's funeral, maybe? I don't know. It doesn't matter right now. I wipe the tears from my eyes and replace the lid on the cup. As I continue walking back to my station, I hear gunshots nearby and am reminded, despite my breaking heart, if I may co-opt the term, this is what's best. This is what will keep him safe.

*

"Hey, can you move?"

I flinch and look at the young lady standing behind me. I am once again in the coffee shop at 3rd and Jordan. The woman standing there is impatient and holding some iced monstrosity with way too much whipped cream on it. "Are you glitching out or something?" she asks.

"No, sorry." I step aside and let her pass. I, likewise, exit the coffee shop and head toward my car. As I do, I take a sip of my latte then throw it in the trash.

I think I'm done with coffee.

About the Author

A.J. Bass was born and raised in the mostly fine state of Indiana. That's not a knock on her home either; it's just that no place is perfect. But, still, it's nice enough that she and her family continue to reside there today.

A.J. got her start in writing when she was in junior high, creating terrible, embarrassing fanfiction that has never and will never see the light of day. In high school, her writing became less terrible, but still remained between herself and her notebooks, and resides (along with the really bad stuff) in a box in her closet labeled "To Be Incinerated Upon My Death." By the time she turned thirty, her writing was at long last deemed fit for general consumption and that was that.

When she's not writing, A.J. likes wandering around graveyards and watching scary movies but doesn't actually believe in ghosts— which comes as a major disappointment to the one who lives in her basement. On warm evenings, she can usually be found outside with her husband, grilling dinner, or walking the neighborhood with her two children looking for random cats to pet; never mind she has two perfectly good cats of her own to pet, already.

Follow A.J. on Twitter @AnjikoZ or on Facebook @AJBassAuthor